"In those ridiculous shoes you're wearing you couldn't make it through one centimeter of snow, never mind close to ten."

"Ten. No, that's impossible," Maggie gasped, adding with a glower, "And will you please stop criticizing my shoes? Just because you don't like them."

Finn turned around, subjecting her to the full force of a look of such intense sensuality that it made her moan out loud.

"I never said anything about not liking them," he told her succinctly. "I simply said that they were impractical."

"*Ridiculous* was the word you used," Maggie reminded him.

As she turned toward the door, she heard Finn saying softly, "I was wrong. Neither ridiculous nor impractical is the right description for them. But provocative—now, that *is*."

PENNY JORDAN has been writing for almost twenty years and has an outstanding record— over one hundred novels published, including *Power Play*, which hit the *New York Times* bestseller lists, and more recently, the phenomenally successful *To Love, Honor and Betray*. With over 60 million copies of her books in print worldwide and translations in more than seventeen languages, Penny Jordan has established herself as an internationally acclaimed author. She was born in Preston, in Lancashire, England, and now lives with her husband in a beautiful fourteenth-century house in rural Cheshire.

Books by Penny Jordan

PROLOGUE

THE head of the Perfect Matches Department, English Speaking Division, scratched the top of his wing in irritation.

'Now look what's happened,' he complained to his newest and least experienced recruit. 'They've called a summit meeting of all the top angels in Cupid Department to discuss the current state of romance. Far too many people are refusing to fall in love and make commitments. If this continues we shall be out of business and a fine thing that would be. Of course they would call this wretched conference when I'm already short-staffed and I've just finished drawing up this session's list of ideally matched pairs. It's too late to put things on hold now, and besides—' he glowered darkly '—this session I'm determined that we're going to meet our target, I am not having that pompous idiot from the Third Agers Section telling me yet again that he's matched up more couples than us. But there's just no one to do the work.'

'There's me.' His newest assistant reminded him eagerly.

The head of the department sighed as he studied the hopeful smile of his trainee recruit. Enthusiasm for one's job was all very well, and to be applauded of course, but in this particular recruit's case that enthusiasm needed to be tempered by the caution of experience and time. However, right now... Right now he had six couples to get together: couples who as yet had no idea that they were meant for one another, couples whose romances needed to be set in motion asap.

Reluctantly he acknowledged that on this occasion he would have to bow to expediency and ignore his forebodings. Handing over his carefully compiled list, he told his junior 'Every one of these couples has been carefully vetted and checked for compatibility. In this department we do not put couples together unless we are sure they will stay together. Everything is set in place and nothing can go wrong. All you have to do is make sure that each and every one of them is in the right place at the right time. You must follow my instructions exactly. No experimentation or short cuts. Do you understand?'

All students had to learn, of course, but it was, to say the least, unfortunate that this particular student's experimentation had led to a New York socialite's pedigree chow falling desperately in love with her neighbour's prize-winning Burmese cat. Luckily the outcome had not been totally without merit, and the marriage which had ensued between the socialite and her neighbour had been a very satisfactory conclusion to the whole affair. He had been working towards pairing her off with someone very different, but there you are...

* * *

'Hi there. What are you doing?'

The new recruit grimaced as one of the naughtiest zephyrs blew playfully on his wings.

'I'm busy,' he responded loftily. 'So go away and bother someone else.'

With hindsight he acknowledged that it had probably been the wrong thing to say. It was common knowledge that this particular zephyr positively enjoyed her reputation for boisterous behaviour, and perhaps it was silly of him to have spread out all the head of department's carefully written notes and instructions, along with the slips on which the names of the humans they related to were written.

'Go away like this, do you mean?' she challenged him, taking a deep breath and sending all his precious papers flying as she exhaled noisily over them.

Of course afterwards she was contrite, and helped him to gather everything up. It was surprising just how much power there was in that ethereal frame, and by the time they had finally collected everything he was feeling out of breath himself.

But that was nothing to the feeling of dread filling him as he tried frantically to remember which couples had been paired together.

The zephyr did what she could, and in the end he was as sure as he could be that he knew what he was supposed to do.

'So, which couple are you going to do first?' she asked him.

He took a deep breath. 'This one,' he told her, showing her their names.

She frowned as she looked at the names and their addresses. 'But how are they going to meet?' she asked him.

'I don't know,' he admitted. 'I'll think of something.'

'Can I help?' she begged eagerly. This was so much more fun than blowing a few leaves off trees, which was all she was ever allowed to do.

'No,' he denied firmly, quickly changing his mind when he saw her taking another deep breath.

As a first step in bringing the two ideally matched partners together, his job was to engineer a meeting between them according to the instructions he had been left.

Engineer a meeting... Right...

CHAPTER ONE

MAGGIE stared in disbelief at the downpour which had suddenly appeared out of nowhere, turning the road she had been driving along into a vast puddle and making her head ache with the tension of concentrating. From the moment she had seen the sale advertised she had been determined to buy the house. She was sure that it was exactly what her adored grandmother needed to lift her out of her current unhappiness.

Of course Maggie knew that nothing and no one could ever replace her grandfather in her grandmother's life, but Maggie was convinced that returning to live in the house where her grandparents had started their married life, a house that was filled with memories of their shared love, would help to take her grandmother's mind off the sadness of her loss. And Maggie was a woman who, once her mind was made up about anything or anyone, refused to change it. Which was why she was such a successful businesswoman—successful enough to be able to attend the auction being held to sell off the large Shropshire estate on which her grandparents had begun their married lives, in the rented house which was now being auctioned for sale.

Maggie had grown up hearing stores of Shropshire and its rich farmlands, but Maggie was a city girl; farms, rain, mud, animals, farmers—they were not for her. The company she owned and ran as a headhunter, her modern city apartment, her friends—single career woman like her—these were the things she enjoyed and valued. But her love for her grandparents was something else, something special. They had provided her with a secure and loving home when her own parents had split up, they had encouraged and praised her, supported her emotionally, loved her, and it both hurt and frightened her to see her once strong grandmother looking so frail and lost.

Until Maggie had seen the Shopcutte estate advertised for sale—its Georgian mansion, farmlands and estate properties, including the pretty Dower House where her grandparents had spent the first years of their marriage— she had been in despair, not knowing how to lift her grandmother's spirits and terrified, if she was honest, that she might actually lose her. But now she knew she had found the perfect means of cheering her up. It was imperative that she was successful at the sale auction, that she acquired the house. And she was determined that she would.

But for this appalling and unforecasted torrential rain she would have reached her destination by now—the small country town adjacent to the estate, where the auction was to be held and where she had booked herself a room at the town's only decent hotel.

When the rain had first started, appearing from nowhere out of a hitherto cloudless sky, she had had to slow her speed down to a crawl. The sky was far from blue now, in fact it was nearly black, and the road was empty of any other traffic as it narrowed and dipped at a perilously acute angle.

Was this really the A-class road she had been following? Impossible, surely, that she might have made a wrong turning. She simply did not do things like that. If there was one thing that Maggie prided herself on it was being in control.

From the top of her glossily groomed, perfectly cut blonde hair to the tips of her equally perfectly pedicured and painted toes Maggie epitomised feminine elegance and self-discipline. Her size eight figure was the envy of her friends—and that flawless skin, that equally flawless personal life, as devoid of the untidiness of emotional entanglements as Maggie's home was devoid of clutter. Yes, Maggie was a woman to be reckoned with: a woman no man would dare not to respect or would risk tangling antagonistically with. After seeing the havoc and mess caused by her parents' various sexual and emotional relationships, Maggie had decided that she intended to remain safely and tidily single. And so far none of the many men she had met had done anything to make her change that decision.

'But you are far too gorgeous to be alone,' one would-be suitor had told her, only to be given one of her most scathing and dismissive looks.

Perhaps somewhere deep down inside herself she did sometimes secretly wonder just why she should be so immune to the dangerous intensity of emotional and physical desire experienced by other women, but she refused to allow herself to dwell on such thoughts. Why should she? She was happy the way she was. Or at least she would be once she had got this auction out of the way and was the owner of the Dower House.

It was ridiculous that she should have had to come out here at all, she fumed as she began a steep descent. She had tried to buy the house prior to the auction, but the agent had refused to sell it. So here she was, and...

'Oh, no. I don't believe it,' she protested out loud as the road turned sharply and she saw in front of her a sign marked 'Ford'.

Ford...as in fording a river, as in some archaic means of crossing it surely more suitable to the Middle Ages rather than the current century. But that was what the sign said, and there in front of her was a shallow river, with the road running right through it and up the hill on its opposite side.

And this was an A road? Irritably Maggie started to drive through the water. That was the country for you, she fumed grittily.

She could hear above the noise of her car engine a loud rushing sound that for some reason made the hair at the back of her neck prickle, and then she saw why. Coming towards her at an unbelievable speed along the course of the river was a wall of water almost as high as the car itself.

For the first time in her life, Maggie panicked. The car's wheels spun as she depressed the accelerator, but the car itself didn't move, and the wall of water...

* * *

Finn was not in a good mood. His meeting had taken much longer than he had planned and now he was going to be late getting back. His mind was preoccupied with his own thoughts, so it gave him a shock to see the unfamiliar car motionless in the middle of the ford, but it gave him even more of a shock to see the swollen race of river threatening to overwhelm it.

He was in no mood to rescue unwanted and uninvited visitors with no more sense than to try to attempt to cross the river during what had to be the worst cloudburst the area had known in living memory, and in such an unsuitable vehicle. He frowned ominously as he dropped the Land Rover into its lowest gear.

He might have made the fortune which had enabled him to retire from the world of commerce by using what his mentor had once told him was the keenest and shrewdest financial brain he had ever come across, but that world and everything it encompassed was not one he ever wanted to return to. This was his *métiere*—what he wanted. But he wanted it permanently. And the lease on Ryle Farm could not be renewed when it ran out in three months' time, which was why he had decided to bid for the Shopcutte estate. He knew that the house, the land and the other properties were being auctioned off in separate lots, but Finn wanted them all. He wanted and he intended to keep the estate intact, and with it his own privacy.

Protecting his privacy; guarding his solitude was vitally important to Finn, and fortunately, thanks to those hectic years he had spent working as one of the City's most successful money market dealers, he had the financial means to buy that privacy and solitude—in the shape of the Shopcutte estate.

Those people who had known him in his early twenties wouldn't be able to reconcile the man he had been then with the man he was now. He was a decade older now, of course, and in those days... In those days his high earning power had gained him an entrée into a fast-living world of trust fund socialites, models, money and drugs. But, as he had quickly come to discover, it was a world driven by greed and filled with insincerity. He had been too hardheaded to succumb to the easy availability of sex and drugs, but others he had known had not been so wise, or so lucky.

Already disenchanted with what had been going on around him, Finn had been filled with a sense of revulsion for the life he was living after the death of one of his colleagues from an accidental drug overdose. Finn had been openly and brazenly propositioned by girls crazed with need by their addiction, had attended parties thrown by clients where those same girls and the drugs that had ruined their lives had been handed round like sweets. It was a world that valued material wealth and held human beings cheap, and one day Finn had woken up and known that it could no longer be his world.

Perhaps unfairly, he had come to blame big city culture for sins that should have more appropriately been apportioned to his fellow human beings. But his own needs had forced him to question what he really wanted out of life, filling him with a craving for peace and a simpler, cleaner, more natural way of life, as well as a loathing for city life and, if he was honest, a wary hostility towards those who lauded it.

His mother had come from farming stock and he had obviously inherited those genes. He had made his plans, taken a calculated gamble on his own judgement which had netted him a profit that had run into millions. His employers had pleaded with him to stay, telling him he could name his own terms, but he had made his decision. Owning his own land would give him the opportunity to grow organic crops as well as breed cattle and increase his small herd of alpaca.

Unlike Maggie, the moment Finn heard the sound of the water thundering towards the ford he knew what it was, and immediately stopped his Land Rover, cursing under his breath as he realised that the huge flood of water filling the riverbed would mean that the ford would be impassable, even for his sturdy four-wheel drive, and that he would end up being marooned on the wrong side of the river. Angrily he looked at Maggie's car. A trendy, top-of-the-range convertible that only a fool would possibly have attempted to take across a flooded ford.

The dangerously fast-flowing water was halfway up the side of the car—and rising. In another few minutes the car would be in danger of being swept completely away, and its blonde-haired driver with it.

Grimly Finn restarted his own vehicle and drove slowly and carefully through the swilling water towards Maggie, gritting his teeth as he felt the powerful surge of the water buffeting the side of the Land Rover and trying to force it downstream.

In her own car, Maggie could not believe what was happening to her. Things like this simply did not happen…especially not to her. How could she possibly be here, in the middle of a flooding river with water creeping higher and higher? She gave a shocked gasp as the car started to move, slewing sideways. She was going to be swept away completely. She might even drown. But she had seen the Land Rover coming up behind her and told herself that she was panicking unnecessarily. If its driver could cross the ford then so could she. Determinedly she tried to restart her car.

Finn simply could not believe his eyes. As he saw Maggie's shiny blonde hair swing across her face when she leaned forward to restart her car he thought he must be hallucinating. What on earth was she doing? Surely she must realise that her car was not going to start? And even if by some remote chance it did…

Drawing alongside her, he carefully brought the Land Rover to a halt and wound down his window.

Maggie saw what he was doing and gave him a supercilious look, which Finn ignored. He could see now that she was a city woman, and his irritation and exasperation with her grew. Gesturing to her to wind down her own window, he returned her look with darkly bitter dislike.

Initially Maggie had intended to ignore his arrogant command—in the City a woman never responded to overtures from unknown men—but then she felt her car move again.

'What the hell do you think you're doing?' Finn demanded irascibly once Maggie had lowered her window. 'You're driving a car, not a submarine.'

His obvious irritation and contempt infuriated Maggie, who was not used to being verbally mauled by the male sex. Normally her looks alone were enough to guarantee that they treated her gently.

'What I am doing,' she responded acidly, 'is trying to ford the river.'

'In this—a flood?' Finn couldn't keep the ire out of his voice.

'There was no flood when I started to cross,' Maggie retaliated hotly, and then gasped as her car started to move again.

'You're going to have to get out of the car,' Finn told her. Any moment now, he suspected, the car would be completely swept away with her in it, if she didn't move quickly, but he was worried that she would start to panic and make the situation even worse than it already was.

'And how do you suggest I do that?' Maggie asked him with a sharp frostiness icing her voice and her eyes. 'Open the door and swim for it?'

'Too dangerous—the current's too strong,' Finn informed her brusquely, ignoring her attempt at sarcasm. Giving her slender body a brisk inspection, he told her crisply, 'You'll have to climb out through the window; there should be enough room. I'm parked close enough for you to be able to crawl into the back of the Land Rover through the rear passenger window.'

'What? You expect me—?' Maggie was almost lost for words. 'I am wearing a designer suit and a pair of very expensive shoes, and there is no way I am going to ruin them by crawling anywhere—least of all into an extremely muddy Land Rover.'

Finn could feel his blood pressure rising, and along with it his temper. He had never met anyone who had irritated him as much as this impossible woman was doing. 'Well, if you stay where you are it won't just be your shoes you'll be in danger of losing. It could be your life as well—and not just your own. Have you any idea of the—?' Finn broke off as her car rocked with the force of the water buffeting it. He had had enough.

'Move. Now,' he ordered her, and to her own shock Maggie found that even before he had finished speaking she was scrambling through her car window.

The feel of two strong male hands supporting her, almost heaving her towards the Land Rover's open window as though she were a...a sack of potatoes, only increased her sense of outrage. As she wriggled and slipped head-first into the rear of the Land Rover the breath whooshed out of her lungs at precisely the same time as her shoes slid off her feet.

Without even having the courtesy to check that she was all right her rescuer was continuing to cross the river, his vehicle somehow pushing its way through the flood which had threatened her own car. As she struggled to sit up Maggie saw her car start to move downstream as the flooding river finally overwhelmed it. She was shivering with shock and reaction, but the driver of the Land Rover seemed totally unconcerned about her as they finally emerged onto dry land and he started to drive up the hill.

Another few seconds and that idiotic woman would have been swept away with her car, Finn fumed once he had safely negotiated their passage back onto dry land. Now, until the river went down, the farm was effectively marooned. There was no other road off the property, which was enclosed on both sides by steep hills.

'You can drop me in the centre of the town,' Maggie informed him in a dismissive clipped voice. 'Preferably opposite a shoe shop, since I now have no shoes.' And not anything else, she recognised. No luggage, no handbag, no credit cards...

'The centre of *what*?' Finn demanded incredulously. 'Where the hell do you think you are?'

'On the A road, five or so miles from Lampton,' Maggie told him promptly.

'On an A road... Does this look like an A road?' Finn's voice was loaded with male disbelief.

Now that she looked at it—properly—Maggie could see that it didn't. For one thing it was barely more than single track, which meant...which meant that somehow or other she must have taken a wrong turning. But she never took wrong turnings—in any area of her life.

'Things are different in the country,' she informed Finn contentiously. 'Any old road can be an A road.'

Her arrogance infuriated him.

'For your information this is a private road, leading only to a farm...my farm.'

Maggie's soft brown eyes widened. She studied the back of Finn's head whilst she tried to assimilate what he had told her. He had a strong bone structure, and thick, very dark brown hair. His hair needed cutting. It covered the collar of his shirt. She wrinkled her nose fastidiously as she took in the shabbiness of his worn coat. She could almost see the forcefield of male anger and hostility that surrounded him, and she felt equally antagonistic towards him.

'So I must have made a wrong turning somewhere.' She gave a small shrug. Only she knew just how much it cost her to admit that she might have got something wrong.

'If you hadn't virtually hijacked me I would have been able to turn round and—'

'Turn round?' Finn interrupted her with a derisive snort. 'If I hadn't turned up you'd have been damned lucky to be alive right now.'

The brutality of his harsh words sent a shiver running through her, but Maggie refused to let him see it. Instead she did what she had trained herself to do, which was to focus on her ultimate goal and ignore everything else.

'How long will it be before the river goes down?' she asked him. 'If we wait here?'

'Wait...?' Finn couldn't keep the disbelief out of his voice. 'Lady, a river like this could take days to subside,' he told her, impatient of her naivety. People like her shouldn't be let loose in the country. They had as much idea of how dangerous nature could be as a child had of crossing a motorway.

'Days…?'

In his driving mirror Finn saw the panic flaring briefly in Maggie's eyes, and against his will he wondered what had caused it. What the hell was he doing, getting curious about her?

'How…how many days?' Maggie asked, fighting not to betray her concern.

Finn shrugged. 'That depends. The last time we had a flood like this it was well over a week.'

'A week…' Now there was no hiding the despair in Maggie's voice. And, if the road really did lead only to the man's farm, it looked as if she had no choice but to spend that week with *him*.

They were almost at the top of the hill now, and automatically she turned round in her seat to look back the way they had come. The Tarmac glistened wetly, a narrow black ribbon against the autumn landscape, and as for her car—she could just about see its roof above the floodwater as it lay at an angle, wedged against a tree.

With the initial shock of what had happened over, Maggie was filled with unfamiliar panic and anxiety. Her clothes, her mobile phone, her bag—with her money and credit cards and all those taken-for-granted things that reaffirmed who and what she was—had gone, swept away from her by the flood with her car. She was, she recognized with stomach-dropping resentment, totally dependent on her rescuer.

In his rearview mirror Finn carefully monitored the

emotions shadowing Maggie's eyes. He knew how to read people, and how to second-guess their thoughts; city life had taught him that. City life, like this city woman. What was a woman like this one doing in such an out-of-the-way country area? Everything about her screamed that she was not a country-lover. And every instinct he had was telling him that she was trouble.

Finn knew danger when he saw it, right enough, but for some reason he couldn't understand he had an overwhelming urge to go ahead and walk right into it, he recognised, with a grim disbelief at his own totally uncharacteristic behaviour as he heard himself saying, 'If you've got friends in the area you can ring them from the farm to tell them what's happened.'

What the hell was he doing, practically inviting her to involve him in her life? Finn asked himself angrily. There was no way he wanted to be there. She irritated and antagonised him to the point where... To the point where he just knew he had to take her in his arms and see if that deliciously full soft mouth felt as good as it looked.

Finn clenched his jaw. What the hell was happening to him? To think...to imagine...to want... He shook his head, appalled by the sheer inappropriateness of his unwelcome thoughts.

'I'm not visiting friends,' Maggie denied tersely.

Finn waited, expecting her to elaborate, and then when she didn't wondered why he should find her refusal to confide in him so intensely aggravating. By rights he should have been pleased that she was so determined to keep her distance from him.

Maggie could feel herself starting to bristle with irritation as she recognised that her rescuer was expecting her to tell him what she was doing in Shropshire. As though she was a child being called to account by an adult. Well, her business was none of his, and besides, the very nature of Maggie's career meant that secrecy and discretion were of prime importance—so much so that they were now second nature to her. Anyway, why should she divulge her very private reasons for being in the area to this...this farmer?

They had crested the hill now, and the lane narrowed even more ahead of them, meandering through pastureland towards a pretty Tudor farmhouse. A small herd of animals grazing in one of the fields was disturbed by the Land Rover and raced away from the fence, capturing Maggie's bemused attention.

'What are those? Llamas?' she asked, unable to check her curiosity.

'No, llamas are much larger. These are alpaca. I keep them for their wool.'

'Their wool?' Maggie repeated, watching as the small herd stopped and one of its braver members craned its long neck to stare at them.

'Yes, their wool,' Finn repeated, adding sardonically, 'It's highly prized and very expensive—and I wouldn't be surprised if your 'designer' hasn't used it in his clothes.'

The way he'd said the word 'designer' was so challenging that Maggie itched to retaliate, but before she could do so he had put the Land Rover in a higher gear and switched on the radio, so that any attempt she might have made to talk would have been drowned out by the sound of the announcer.

'Sounds like we're not the only ones to be caught out by this freak storm,' Finn commented.

'Thank you,' Maggie told him tartly. 'But I don't need a translation. I do speak English.'

The auction was in six days time—the river had to have gone back to normal by then. She wished now that she had not given herself this extra time, but she had hoped to be able to convince the agent, when she talked with him face to face, to accept her offer for the Dower House prior to the auction taking place. She was fully prepared to pay, and to pay generously to secure the house. Anything to see her grandmother smile again.

They were driving into the farmyard now—in the paddock beyond it Maggie could see hens scratching in the grass and ducks on the pond. An idyllic scene, no doubt, to some people. But not to her, no way, and especially not when it came inhabited by a man like the one who was now turning round in his seat towards her.

'Let's just get one thing straight,' he was telling her grimly, 'I don't like this situation any more than you do, and, moreover, I was not the one who stupidly drove my car into a river which was plainly in full flood. Neither was I the one who made a wrong turning and ended up—'

'There was no flood when I tried to cross the ford,'

Maggie interrupted him sharply. 'It just seemed to come out of nowhere—as though…' As though some malign fate had been waiting for her, she wanted to say, but of course she was far too sensible to make such a silly comment. 'And, since you apparently own this wretched place, I should have thought you would have a legal obligation to warn motorists of just how dangerous it is to use the supposed ford.'

Ignoring her mistaken belief that he owned the farm—this was no time to become involved in minor details—Finn barred his teeth savagely in an unfriendly smile whilst he reminded Maggie unkindly, 'Since this road is private, and on privately owned land, there isn't any need.'

'That's all very well,' Maggie countered immediately, 'but perhaps you could explain to me just how a person is supposed to know that, if there isn't a sign to tell them so?'

'There doesn't need to be a sign,' Finn told her through gritted teeth. 'It's perfectly plain from any map that this is virtually a single-track road which leads to a dead end. Women,' he exploded sardonically. 'Why is it they seem pathologically incapable of reading maps?'

Maggie had had enough—all the more so because of the small inner logical voice that was trying to tell her unwantedly that her adversary had a point.

'I can read a map perfectly well, thank you, and I can read human beings even better. You are the rudest, most arrogant, most…irritating man I have ever met,' she told him forcefully.

'And you are the most impossible woman I have ever met,' Finn retaliated.

Silently they looked at one another in mutual hostility.

CHAPTER TWO

MAGGIE finished the call she had just made to her assistant explaining to her what had happened and asking her to organise the cancellation and reissue of her credit cards.

'Do you want them sent direct to you where you are?' Gayle had asked her.

'Er, no... Get them to send them to the hotel for me instead, please Gayle. Oh, and when you report what's happened to my insurance company and the garage make sure they know I'm going to need a courtesy car, will you?'

She had kept the details of what had happened brief, cutting through Gayle's shocked exclamations after she had retreated to the room Finn Gordon had shown her to, clutching the mobile telephone he had loaned her. It galled her to have to ask him for anything, and she frowned now as she quickly dialled her grandmother's number. She hadn't told her what she was planning to do, had simply fibbed instead that she was going away on business for a few days.

The fraility in Arabella Russell's voice when she answered Maggie's call choked Maggie's own voice with emotion.

* * *

Standing outside the partially open door, with the cup of tea he had made for his unexpected and unwanted guest, Finn heard the soft liquid note of love in her voice as she asked, 'Are you all right, darling?'

Stepping back sharply from the door, he wondered why the knowledge that there was a man, a lover in Maggie's life should be so unwelcome.

They had exchanged names earlier, with a reluctance and formality which in other circumstances he would have found ruefully amusing. Despite her bedraggled state, Maggie still managed to look far too desirable for his comfort. He had tried to reassure himself that his preference was and always had been for brunettes, and that he preferred blue eyes to brown, but he had still found himself staring at her for just that little bit too long.

Her call to her grandmother over, Maggie examined her surroundings. The room Finn had shown her to was large, and mercifully possessed its own bathroom. Its dormer windows looked out onto fields, beyond which lay some awesomely steep hills clothed in trees. The autumn light was already fading. What on earth was she going to do, stuck here until the river subsided? Maggie wondered bitterly.

Her request to her 'host' for access to his computer so that she could e-mail Gayle had met with a grim and uncompromising, 'I don't have one. I prefer to choose whom I allow to intrude into my life.'

Which had been a dig at her as well as a reinforcement

of his dislike of technology, Maggie suspected. The man was positively Neanderthal. Everyone had a computer. Everyone, that was, but this farmer she had managed to get herself trapped with. Crossly Maggie acknowledged that if fate had done it deliberately to annoy her it couldn't have produced a man who would antagonise and irritate her more, or whose lifestyle was so much the opposite of hers. So far as she was concerned the river could not go down fast enough—and not just because of the impending auction.

In his kitchen, Finn was listening to the local weather forecast on the radio. As yet no one had been able to come up with any an explanation for the freak storm that had been so oddly localised and which, it seemed, had caused chaos which was only limited to within a few miles of the farm.

Finn hoped the river would be crossable in time for the auction. He preferred to bid in person rather than by phone; he liked to see the faces of his competitors so that he could gauge their strengths and weaknesses. Not that he was expecting to have much competition for the estate so far as the main house and the agricultural land went. However, when it came to the estate cottages it was a different matter. There was no way he wanted second home owners or holidaymakers living on his land. No, what he wanted was his privacy. What he wanted—

He turned round as the kitchen door opened and Maggie walked in. She had removed the jacket of her suit and the thin silk blouse she was wearing revealed the soft swell of her breasts, surprisingly well rounded in such an otherwise fragile fine-boned woman. The sight of her in silk shirt, plain gold earrings and straight tailored black skirt, but minus her shoes, caused Finn to smile slightly.

Immediately her chin came up, her eyes flashing warningly. 'One word,' she cautioned him. 'Just one word and I'll...'

Finn couldn't resist. 'You'll what?' he goaded her. 'Throw something at me? A shoe, perhaps?'

'I'm a mature woman,' Maggie told him through gritted teeth. 'I do not throw things...ever.'

'What? Not even caution to the winds, in the arms of your lover?' Finn derided her. 'How very disappointing that must be for him.'

Maggie couldn't believe her ears. How on earth had they managed to get on such personal ground?

'I do not have a lover,' she heard herself telling Finn sharply.

Finn digested her too-quick denial with silent cynicism. He already knew that she was lying. She embodied everything he most disliked about the life he had left behind him. So why did he feel this virtual compulsion just to stand and look at her? He had seen more beautiful women, and he had certainly known far more sexually encouraging women. She had an almost visible ten-foot-high fence around her, warning him to keep his distance—which was exactly what he wanted and intended to do. So why was a reckless part of him hungrily wondering what it would feel like to hold her, to kiss her, to…?

Compressing his mouth against the folly of such thoughts, he said curtly, 'I'm going out to lock up the fowl for the night. If you want something to eat help yourself from the fridge.'

Help herself? Eat on her own? Well, he certainly believed in being hospitable, Maggie reflected waspishly as she watched him walk out into the yard. If she'd been in the City now she would still have been working. She rarely finished work before eight, often leaving her office even later, and most evenings she either had dinner with clients or friends; if with friends at one of the City's high-profile restaurants, if with clients somewhere equally expensive but far more discreet.

Her apartment possessed a state-of-the-art stainless steel kitchen, but Maggie had never cooked in it. She could cook, of course. Well, sort of. Her grandmother was a wonderful cook and had always encouraged Maggie to concentrate on her studies whilst she was growing up, and somehow there had never been time for Maggie to learn domestic skills from her.

Well, at least if she had something to eat now she could retreat to her room and stay there. Who knew? By tomorrow the river might be fordable again. Certainly if it was possible for a person to will that to happen then that person would be Maggie.

Skirting the large table in the middle of the room, she looked disparagingly at the untidy mess of books and papers cluttering it. An old-fashioned chair complete with a snoozing cat was pulled up in front of the Aga, not a bright shiny new Aga, Maggie noticed, but an ancient chipped cream one. The whole house had a run-down air about it, a sad shabbiness that evoked feelings in her she didn't want to examine.

Maggie had spent the early years of her childhood being dragged from one set of rented lodgings to another by her mother after the break-up of her parents' marriage. Every time her mother had met a new man they had moved, and inevitably, when the romance ended, they had moved again. In some people such a life might have created a deep-seated need for stability and the comfort and reassurance of a close loving relationship with a partner, in Maggie it had created instead a ferocious determination to make herself completely and totally independent.

This house reminded her of those days and that life and she didn't like it. Nothing in Maggie's life now—the life she had created for herself—was shabby or needy, nothing was impermanent or entered into impulsively without cautious and careful thought. Everything she surrounded herself with was like her: shiny, clean, groomed, planned, ordered and controlled.

Or rather like she normally was, she corrected herself, as she looked down at her unshod feet in their expensive designer tights. Maggie never went barefoot—not even in the privacy of her own home—and most certainly never in anyone else's home. To her being barefoot was surely synonymous with being poor, and vulnerable, and either of those things made her feel weak and afraid and angry with herself for feeling that way.

Quickly she went to open the fridge door. She was becoming far too dangerously introspective. As she looked into the fridge her eyes widened.

Finn pushed open the back door and removed his boots. The paddock was a quagmire of mud, partially due to the activities of the ducks and partially to the recent downpour. He had had the devil of a time catching one of the bantams, and had even got to the point of consigning the little wretch to the devil and the nightly marauding fox, but in the end his inherent concern for its safety had won out and he had persevered, finally managing to lock it up safely.

He was cold and hungry and his afternoon's unscheduled meeting with the alpaca breeder had meant that he hadn't made the chilli he had intended to prepare for his supper. He had an evening's worth of paperwork in front of him, which he wasn't looking forward to. Perhaps he was making life harder for himself than it needed to be by refusing to install a computer. It would certainly make his paperwork easier.

As he kicked off his muddy boots he could see Maggie staring into the open fridge.

'What's wrong?' he demanded as he walked across to her.

'Everything in here's raw,' Maggie responded in consternation. Like him, she was hungry, and had somehow been expecting...well, if not the kind of meal that would be served at one of London's stylish restaurants, then at least a pizza.

An answering frown of disapproval furrowed Finn's own forehead, as he listened to her.

'What else did you expect? This is a farm, not a supermarket,' he told her dryly. 'We live at the beginning of the food chain, not at its end.'

'But it all needs cooking,' Maggie protested. She was looking at him with a mixture of hauteur and disdain that made Finn long to shake her.

'Look, this isn't some fancy city restaurant; of course it needs cooking.'

To his astonishment Maggie slammed the fridge door shut and stepped back from it. 'I've decided that I'm not hungry,' she told him coolly.

'Well, no, I don't suppose you are. You look as though you don't live on much more than a few overrated radicchio leaves,' Finn told her unkindly.

Maggie wasn't sure what infuriated her most, his contempt for her figure or his contempt for her lifestyle. And anyway, how did a man like him know to name the City's current of-the-moment salad ingredient? Maggie wondered sourly.

'Well, you may not be hungry, but I most certainly am,' he told her, reaching past her to re-open the fridge door.

At such close quarters Maggie could actually feel the male heat coming off his body as well as see its unwantedly disturbing male strength. What on earth was the matter with her? She had never been the kind of woman who had been interested in or affected by the sight of a well-defined muscular torso. And he had the kind of facial bone structure that any male model would pay a plastic surgeon thousands for, she decided unkindly, driven by a raw need to somehow punish him for making her aware of him at all, even if it was only in the privacy of her own thoughts. He was all taut male planes and angles, and as for his eyes—surely it was impossible for a man with such dark brown hair to have such shockingly dangerous steel-blue eyes?

'Changed your mind?' she heard Finn asking her.

'What...? I...?' As she started to stammer with unfamiliar self-consciousness she wondered how on earth he could have guessed that she was unexpectedly being forced to revise her first impression of him as a man she found physically unappealing, despite his good looks.

'You look hungry,' Finn explained patiently.

She looked hungry! Maggie felt her face start to burn, and then realised that Finn couldn't possibly mean what she had thought he meant, that he couldn't possibly know what she was thinking and feeling...yes, feeling... For a man she hardly knew—a man she didn't want to know. What on earth was happening to her? The thoughts she was having—they were...they were impossible, inadmissible, unthinkable. But as they stood facing one another, with the fridge door open between them, the most peculiar feeling was sweeping over Maggie, an odd sort of light-headedness combined with an awareness of Finn as a man in the most shockingly intimate sort of way, so shocking, in fact, that—Maggie shook her head, trying to dispel her riotously erotic thoughts, her face growing pink at their temerity and inventiveness. This was totally alien to her. She had never before imagined, dreamed, nor wanted to imagine or dream such things, such needs, such desires. Even the air she was breathing seemed to be filled with a sense of urgency and excitement—of expectation, almost—that she was totally at a loss to understand. It was almost as though someone or something outside herself was forcing her to see Finn in a different light...

Finn's eyes narrowed assessingly as he saw Maggie's pupils dilate. She had started to breathe more quickly, her lips parting, her breasts rising and falling in a way that made it impossible for him not to be aware of her femininity. He had the most extraordinarily intense desire to close the fridge door and to take her in his arms and...

Grimly he turned away from her.

'I intended to cook a chilli for my own supper; there'll be more than enough for two.'

He sounded curtly dismissive, as though he was secretly hoping she would refuse. Well, tough—why should she? She wasn't going to go to bed supperless just to please some arrogant, impossible man. No way.

'I take it you won't be cooking dinner wearing that?' she said tartly, determined to wrest control of the situation into her own domain as she flicked a deliberately disparaging glance at his ancient coat.

The look Finn gave her sent a prickle of alluring excitement that was totally alien to her racing down her spine.

'No, I won't be,' he agreed, his voice mock affable as he added carelessly, 'In fact you could get the chilli started whilst I go up and have a shower. Here's the mince,' he informed her as he removed a covered container from the bottom of the fridge. 'I shan't be long.'

Helplessly Maggie stared at the container he had given her before going over to the worktop and reluctantly opening it. What she should have done was tell him in no uncertain terms before he had left the kitchen that there was no way she was going to be turned into some kind of unpaid domestic help and that he could make his own supper. But, having missed that opportunity to put him in his place and save her own face, she had no option other than to try to cook the wretched stuff. There was no way, not ever in a hundred years, a thousand years, that she was going to admit to him that she had no idea how to cook it.

Anyway, it couldn't be that difficult, could it? She had seen her grandmother cooking whilst she worked on her homework at the kitchen table. It was surely just a matter of putting it in a pan and... Her forehead furrowed into a frown of concentration as she tried to remember just what her grandmother had done, mentally picturing her in the comfortable kitchen of the home that she had made Maggie's. She could visualise her grandmother plainly enough, smiling, bustling between the cooker and the sink whilst delicious mouthwatering smells filled the room. But as to what she had actually been doing...

Maggie mentally squared her shoulders. She could do it. She had to do it. There was no way she would ever concede victory to that...that farmer.

She needed a pan first, and the logical place for that had to be in a cupboard close to the Aga. Pleased with her own intelligence, she went towards it.

Five minutes later, when she had checked every cupboard in the kitchen, red-faced and fuming, she finally found what she was looking for on the opposite side of the room. And men had the audacity to claim that women were illogical. Ha!

Decanting the contents of the container into the pan, she grimaced in distaste. It looked unappealingly raw. She carried the pan over to the Aga and stood nonplussed in front of it before tentatively lifting one of the covers. The heat coming off the hotplate made her wince before hastily putting the pan down on it and stepping back. Now all she had to do was to wait for the stuff to cook. Good.

Upstairs in his bedroom, Finn rubbed his damp hair dry and then dropped the towel to reach for a clean shirt to pull over his naked torso. He didn't want to analyse why he had found it necessary not just to shower but to shave as well, and he wasn't going to.

A pungent smell was beginning to fill the air. He sniffed it warily and then frowned. Something was burning. Without bothering to put on his shirt, he made for the door.

In the kitchen, Maggie couldn't understand what was happening. A horrid pall of smoke was filling the room—and as for the smell! The mince couldn't be cooked yet, surely? She had a memory, admittedly vague, of her grandmother spending far longer than a mere few minutes cooking hers!

Cautiously she approached the Aga, and was just about to lift the lid off the pan when Finn came bursting into the kitchen.

'What the hell are you doing?' he was demanding as he strode past her and grabbed the pan off the stove, carrying it over to the sink, where he dumped it unceremoniously then removed its lid to peer in disgust at its smoking contents before turning on the tap.

'It's not my fault if your cooker isn't reliable,' Maggie informed him with a bravado she was far from feeling.

'My cooker!' Finn exclaimed through gritted teeth. 'It isn't the cooker that's unreliable, it's the cook. Why on earth didn't you add some more water to it?'

Some *more* water. Maggie gulped and looked away, feigning disdain, but obviously her acting wasn't good enough, because to her chagrin she heard Finn saying in an oh, so dangerously soft voice, 'You did add water, didn't you?'

Maggie swallowed. Her grandmother had had very strong views about lying, but surely on this occasion...

'You didn't, did you?' Finn breathed in disbelief.

Maggie affected a nonchalant shrug. 'So we favour different schools of cooking…'

'Different schools?' His eyes narrowed. 'You haven't a clue, have you?' He scoffed sardonically. 'Thank you, fate. Not only have I got to house her; I've got to feed her as well. Tell me,' he invited unkindly, 'just how many other non-skills do you possess that are likely to bring havoc to my life? You can't read a map, you can't cook, you—'

'Stop it.'

Maggie wasn't sure which of them was the more shocked by the sound of her tear-filled voice.

The silence it caused seemed to stretch for ever, hostility giving way to shock, shock to a soft little prickle of sensual tension which in turn led…

'I'm sorry.' It was the gruff note of real apology in Finn's voice that did it, Maggie assured herself later. That and the fact that she had really been intending to walk past him and out of the room—would have walked past him if her eyes hadn't been blurred by tears of shame and anger causing her instead to walk into him, into him and into…into his arms.

CHAPTER THREE

'I'M SORRY. I didn't mean to hurt you,' Finn apologised gruffly, as he pushed the silky hair back off Maggie's face, his fingertips enjoying the soft delicacy of her skin. Her throat seemed to fit the curve of his hand perfectly. She was trembling slightly, and in his own body...

'You haven't. You didn't,' Maggie responded huskily. She couldn't stop looking at him; their glances were meeting, meshing, mating; she didn't want to stop looking at him.

'I'll make us something else to eat,' Finn offered. He knew he should release her, but he didn't want to, couldn't bear to.

Maggie shook her head. 'It's you I'm hungry for,' she whispered softly. 'Not food. Just you. Only you, Finn.'

As she lifted her face towards his Maggie knew that she had never done anything in the whole of her life that felt more right than this, more right than Finn.

Finn tried to apply the brakes of caution and common sense to the escalating urgency of his response to her, but one look into the dark haze of her passion-filled eyes had much the same effect on those brakes as the wall of water sweeping down the river had had on Maggie's car.

His kiss was tentative at first, his lips exploring the soft curves of hers, but then she moved closer to him, nestling into his arms, her breathing quickening, the look in her eyes making Finn groan out loud.

'Kiss me, Finn,' Maggie whispered insistently, adding with a shaky urgency that made Finn catch his own breath in fierce longing, 'Properly this time.'

'Like this, do you mean?'

Finn's hand slid beneath her hair, supporting her head as they gazed helplessly at one another. They kissed quickly, as though equally wary of what they were doing, equally wary of their mutual hunger for one another. Brief, fierce kisses were snatched, as though they were starving, in fear of being deprived of the means of satisfying their hunger. But slowly their kisses became longer, deeper.

Behind her closed eyelids, Maggie savoured the richness of the texture of Finn's mouth. His kisses were the most extraordinarily sensual she had ever experienced. Without doing anything more than holding her and kissing her he had made her whole body come alive with longing for him. Everything about him was having the most erotic aphrodisiacal effect on her, making her think things, want things, want him, with a female ardour and urgency that left her breathless. Breathless and aching, eager, hungry, and wanting him. Just as he wanted her. Finn was a man, and even if his kisses hadn't shown her that he wanted her as passionately as she did him his body would have given him away.

Experimentally she slid her tongue-tip into his mouth. The arm he had wrapped around her body tightened and she felt him shudder, felt too the corresponding quiver of reaction that set her own limbs shaking.

'Don't do that unless you mean it,' Finn warned her rawly. Heat flamed in his eyes, and beneath her explorative fingertips the hard high planes of his cheekbones burned.

'I do mean it,' Maggie responded. Automatically she looked round the kitchen, and, correctly sensing what she was seeking, what she was thinking, Finn released her from his arms and took hold of her hand, silently leading her out of the kitchen and towards the stairs.

His bedroom was on the opposite side of the landing to the room he had given her. Silently he drew her into it, and equally silently Maggie went with him. It was simply and traditionally furnished, and at any other time she would have turned her nose up its shabbiness and lack of style. But the bed was large, with heavy iron head and footboards.

The air in the room was clean and slightly cold, so that Maggie shivered a little.

Watching her, Finn remembered how cold he too had found the farmhouse when he had first moved in. It didn't possess any central heating, but he had grown used to its lack of modern conveniences.

As she shivered again Maggie instinctively moved closer to Finn, seeking the warmth of his body. The sensation of his arms closing around her was so intense that it rocked her on her heels. As they kissed Maggie felt as though Finn's warmth was wrapping itself all around her, enfolding her. She could feel his hands moving over her body and she started to tremble. Not with cold now, but with a growing ache of need.

Unable to resist their temptation, Finn explored the taut shape of Maggie's breasts. Her nipples, tight and erect, pressed into his palms through the fine silk of her shirt. Opening his eyes, he absorbed the eroticism of their tautness pushing against the fabric before slowly circling them with his thumb-tip.

Maggie had forgotten that she had ever been cold now. Feverishly she slid her palms over Finn's naked torso. She ached to see all of him. To touch all of him, and now, oh yes, right now.

She had just made the very interesting discovery that when she trailed her fingertips across his collarbone and then down his arm his whole body shuddered in sharp response, and when she placed her hand flat against his chest and then moved it lower, so low that it was resting on the belt of his jeans, that shudder became a whole lot more intense.

His own hand was travelling the length of her spine, taking her mind off the way he was reacting and focusing it instead on the way she was feeling. Arousal, hot and sharp, lifted her skin in tiny goosebumps against his touch, as though it just couldn't get close enough to him.

She exhaled softly as Finn's hand moved to the buttons on her shirt, and then found that the sensation of his fingertips brushing against her naked skin as he unfastened them was making it impossible for her to breathe in again.

As he pulled the fabric back from Maggie's body Finn

acknowledged that what was happening between them was destroying virtually every belief he had about what he wanted from life.

Watching him, and seeing the open, raw male sensuality blazing out of his heavily-lidded eyes, Maggie exhaled.

The feel of her soft sweet breath gusting warmly against his bare skin made Finn grit his teeth against the ferocity of his reaction to her. The air ached with the sexual tension stretching between them.

As Finn leaned forward to kiss first one of her naked breasts and then the other, Maggie moaned sharply, her body arching towards him in mute supplication.

It was too much for Finn's self-control; she was too much for his self-control. Quickly removing the rest of her clothes and his own, Finn lifted Maggie onto the bed.

The coldness of the cotton duvet beneath her bare back made Maggie shiver, but the heat of her desire for Finn soon burned away that cold. Her body throbbed with longing for him, and the feel of his hands on her skin as he lowered himself against her and slid them beneath her to lift her hips to meet his own made her cry out, a wild tormented female sound of need that echoed the turbulence darkening her eyes.

'Finn,' she cried out his name as she wrapped herself around him, pressing wild hot kisses against his skin, his throat, his jaw, his mouth, holding it captive with her own whilst her body shook. 'Now, Finn,' she begged him passionately. 'Now.'

It was the force of the river at full flood, the warmth of the sun on a tropical beach, the cool magical clarity of a frosty sky married to the purity of newly fallen snow; it was every pleasure she had ever know intensified a million times. He filled her body with joy and her heart with an emotion so intense that it spilled from her eyes in pure gleaming tears and from her mouth in a golden sound of loving words. It was a revelation, and somehow an affirmation. It was a world she had always stubbornly refused to believe could exist and at the same time a world a secret part of her had always longed to inhabit. It was. It was Finn and it was love. And as her body came down from the heights his had taken it to and she lay drifting on the soft safe warm afterswell of pleasure, lying at peace in his arms, Maggie turned to look at the man who had just totally changed her life.

Gazing deep into his eyes, she lifted her fingertips to his face, tracing its contours wonderingly. Looking back at her, Finn took her hand and held it against his lips, tenderly kissing her fingers.

'I love you.'

Maggie could see shock followed by an intense burn of emotion darkening Finn's eyes as she said the simple words.

Saying them had shocked her as well—so much so, in fact, that she immediately longed to call them back, wondering frantically why she had ever uttered them, furiously angry with herself for the vulnerability they were now causing her to feel. As though desperate to escape them she tried to turn away from Finn, but he refused to allow her to do so, taking hold of her instead, his hands gentle on the tense resistance of her body.

'What is it? What's wrong?' he asked her quietly.

'Nothing,' Maggie lied sharply as she tried to evade the quiet depth of his searching gaze.

'Yes, there is.' Finn contradicted her. 'You're angry because you said you love me.'

'No,' Maggie denied fiercely, but she could tell from the expression in Finn's eyes that he didn't believe her.

'I don't know why I said it.' She tried to cover herself. 'It must have been some kind of knee-jerk adolescent reaction to the fact that we...'

When she stopped Finn supplied softly for her, 'That we made love? Is that what you're trying to say?'

Maggie shook her head. She had been intending to use the words 'had sex', if for no other reason than to remind herself of just what the reality of their situation was. But something in Finn's eyes had warned her against doing so.

'We're both adults, Maggie,' Finn was telling her gently. 'Why should it be so difficult for us to use the word 'love' about what we've just shared, about one another? There was love between us. And to deny that...'

He paused and shook his head, whilst Maggie, thoroughly unnerved by what he was saying burst out sharply, 'We hardly know one another. We can't.'

'We can't what?' Finn challenged her. 'We can't tell one another that we've fallen in love, even though it's true? We can't mention it? Show it to one another...like this?' And then he was reaching for her, wrapping her in his arms and holding her so tightly that she could hardly breathe as he told her with fierce raw male intensity, 'I don't know how this has happened to us or why, Maggie, but I do know that now that it has...'

As his fingers stroked through her hair Maggie revelled in the mute tenderness of his touch, its confirmation of his admission of love. 'Now that it has what?' she asked him.

'Now that it has...this...' Finn responded.

As he started to kiss her his fingertips slid seductively down her spine. Voluptuously Maggie closed her eyes on a tiny moan of helpless resignation. There would be time later for her to analyse her feelings and get them back under her own control. For now...

For now there was nothing she wanted more than the feel of Finn's flesh against her fingertips, the feel of Finn himself against her.

A triumphant smile curved Maggie's mouth as she lifted the lid from the casserole she had just removed from the Aga and sniffed the delicious aroma emanating from it. For this evening's supper they would be eating *coq au vin,* thanks to the slightly battered cookbook she had unearthed from deep inside one of the kitchen cupboards.

Or chicken casserole, as Finn would no doubt describe it.

Finn. Helplessly, knowing how much she would regret her foolishness and berate herself mentally for it, Maggie closed her eyes and succumbed to the temptation to slowly and lovingly mentally recreate every single inch of him.

Four days ago she hadn't even known he existed, and wouldn't have cared if she had; three days ago she had known, but could have quite definitely contemplated a world without him. But now... Now... A loving dreamy smile softened her mouth, her emotions too powerful for her to ignore. She still felt bemused by the speed with which they had fallen in love—bemused by it when she wasn't desperately trying to remind herself of all the reasons why it was impossible for her to behave in such an irrational and impulsive way, allowing her emotions to control her instead of the other way around—and completely, totally enchanted, enthralled and enraptured by Finn himself.

And somehow, without knowing quite how, and totally against her better judgement, she had allowed Finn to convince her that what they felt for one another was too wonderfully special to be ignored. They were in love. They whispered it to one another in the sleepy relaxed closeness of shared spent passion, moaned it to one another in its tumultuous throes, cried it out to one another as they climbed its heights together, vowed it to one another in barely spoken tender triumphant post orgasmic mutual bliss. They were in love.

Cautiously Maggie had allowed herself to wriggle out of the protective straitjacket of emotional denial she had cocooned herself in for her own safety, to begin to believe in what she was feeling, to make plans...

This morning she had woken up to find Finn leaning over her, his head propped up on one hand whilst he looked at her.

'What is it? What are you doing?' she had asked him sleepily as she reached up to touch the rough stubble on his jaw with one delicate fingertip.

'Watching you,' had been his husky reply. 'Did you know that you twitch your nose when you're asleep?'

'No, I don't,' Maggie had denied.

'Yes, you do,' Finn had told her lovingly. 'And you part your lips just a little, so that I'm irresistibly tempted to kiss them to see if they taste as soft and warm as they look.'

'If you don't know that by now,' Maggie had begun to challenge him teasingly, 'when you've had enough opportunity to find out…'

'No. Never, never, ever could I have enough of you,' Finn had told her, adding with a dangerous glint in his eyes, 'Want me to prove it?'

Laughing, she had pretended to try to escape as he reached for her and wrapped her in his arms.

'Oh, I know it,' Finn had confirmed, giving her a sexily smouldering dark-eyed look that had made her stomach muscles quiver in delicious anticipation. 'And I know too that if I touch you here…' His fingertips had brushed against her already taut nipple and Maggie had raised her hand to his collarbone, tracing its length with fingers that trembled slightly.

It had been gone ten o'clock when they had finally

got up. An appallingly late hour for a farmer, Finn had told her.

He was out checking on the animals now. Soon he would be back, and then...

Maggie replaced the casserole in the Aga, concentrating on the weather forecast being broadcast on the radio.

The freak flood was subsiding, the forecaster announced, and no further cloudbursts were expected.

Which meant—which meant that she would be able to make it to the auction, Maggie decided in relief.

All morning whilst she prepared her *coq au vin* she had been making plans. The farm was only rented, Finn had told her that, which meant that Finn was free to return to the City with her. She closed the Aga door and frowned slightly. It did concern her a little, if she was honest, that a man of Finn's age should only be renting a property—and as for his lack of ambition... But that could be remedied, she felt sure.

He was an intelligent man and she was convinced that with her encouragement and support he could soon gain enough qualifications to get a proper job in the City. Heavens, if she, with her connections, couldn't help him then no one could. And she was fully prepared to support him financially whilst he retrained. It was true that it was a little hard for her to visualise him living in her small apartment, with its minimalistic elegance, but somehow they would manage. She would take him to a suitable shop and get him a decent suit, and then she would organise a get-together at one of her favourite 'in' restaurants so that he could meet her friends, perhaps one or two people with the right connections, so that he could begin networking.

Her mind working busily, Maggie continued to plan. They would have a small elegant wedding—thanks, perhaps, to her grandmother she was old-fashioned enough to want to give their love the commitment of marriage—perhaps at one of the City's newly licensed and breathtakingly beautiful National Trust properties. They would honeymoon somewhere far, far away and ridiculously romantic, and frighten each other by remembering how easily they might not have met.

Happily engrossed in her thoughts, Maggie didn't hear Finn come into the kitchen. Removing his boots, he stood for a few seconds watching her. Was it really only four days ago that he had considered her the most infuriating woman he had ever met? Smiling ruefully, he walked up behind her, wrapping his arms around her as he lowered his head to gently nuzzle the side of her neck.

'Mmm…something smells good,' he told her appreciatively.

'My perfume,' Maggie responded huskily. What was it about that touch of a certain man's lips and only his that had the power to reduce a woman to this state of sweetly intense longing, to make her want to…?

'No, I meant the dinner,' Finn informed her.

Maggie pretended indignation as she leaned back in his arms. 'It said on the radio that the river is going down,' she told him, closing her eyes, wanting to purr with sensuality as his fingertips stroked down her arm and found the deliciously sensitive little spot just inside her elbow where last night the touch of his mouth had made her moan softly with pleasure as her body arched languidly into his.

'Yes, I know. I heard it too,' he confirmed.

Still looking at him with eyes liquid with pleasure, Maggie reluctantly reminded herself of something she had to do. She hadn't been able to speak with her grandmother—her grandmother was used to Maggie going away on business and being incommunicado for a couple of days or so, but Maggie wanted to telephone Gayle and ask her to let her know that she would soon be in touch.

Ringing herself was too fraught with potential hazards for Maggie to contemplate right now. Whilst Arabella Russell had never been the kind of person to sit in judgement on others, nor was someone who believed in imposing her own moral values on them, Maggie wanted to be in a position to explain to her grandmother just how she felt, as well as what had happened, in person. And, just as she did not feel comfortable with her grandmother worrying about what she was doing, neither did she feel comfortable with the prospect of Finn perhaps teasing her for worrying about an old lady's sensibilities.

For an adult woman to be worrying about how her grandmother might react to the fact that she had made love with a man she had only known a matter of hours might seem justifiably risible in this day and age, but Maggie was not going to expose either herself or her grandmother to Finn's potential amusement.

As he watched Maggie's eyes darken and the expressions of concern and anxiety chase one another across her face, Finn was forced to acknowledge what he had determinedly pushed to the back of his mind ever since he'd overheard her phone call that first day. Namely, that he wasn't the only man in Maggie's life. Initially he had told himself that it didn't matter, but of course it did, and it had mattered from the first moment he had kissed her; from the first moment he had wanted to kiss her, he corrected himself grimly.

There was nothing he wanted more than for them to be completely honest with one another. The love he felt for her demanded it. What would happen if he told her that he already knew? Perhaps...

'Finn? May I use your telephone? There's a phone call I need to make.' Maggie could see Finn frowning as she blurted out her request.

'Someone special?' Finn asked her as lightly as he could, inwardly praying that she would open up to him, tell him about the someone else she shared her life with, and tell him too that what *they* now shared meant that her relationship with her existing lover would have to end.

Someone special. Maggie tensed. Her grandmother was special, but she wasn't ready yet to tell Finn about her, or to explain to him just why Arabella Russell mattered so much to her. The caution that had guarded her for so much of her life hadn't entirely lifted its heavy barrier from her heart.

'No...I just need to speak to my...my assistant.'

Finn knew immediately that there was something she

was concealing from him. Silently he prayed that she would tell him what it was before…

Confused, Maggie waited for Finn to answer her. What on earth was it about a simple request to use his telephone that had brought such a darkly brooding look to his face?

There was nothing else for it, Finn acknowledged. If Maggie wasn't going to tell him of her own accord then he was going to have to force the issue, to make his own position plain, put his cards on the table and tell her here and now what he was looking for from their relationship—that nothing less than total and complete commitment from her would satisfy him.

He knew that taking such a step was a gamble, a gamble which would have been dangerous even without the hidden presence of another man in her life, given the brevity of the time they had known one another. Still, it was a gamble he had to take; his love for her was forcing him to take it. He hoped that once Maggie knew just what he wanted from her she would drop her guard and tell him the truth.

Finn took a deep breath, and then, his hands cupping Maggie's shoulders with firmly tender strength, he looked down into her eyes. 'Before you do anything else, speak to anyone else,' he emphasised, hoping she would guess that he knew who it was she really wanted to speak to, 'there's something I have to say to you—something I've never said or wanted to say to any other woman.'

He paused whilst Maggie tried to guess what was

coming, impatient to get her phone call out of the way, let Gayle know that with the river no longer flooding she would soon be back in London, so that she could tell Finn about the exciting plans she had been making for both of them. Plans that meant that the sooner she did get back to the City, the sooner she could be starting to work on the wonderful life they would be sharing together.

'Yes?' she urged Finn curiously. They had already told one another of their love, so it couldn't be that

'I want you to move in here with me, Maggie.'

Finn could see the shock that Maggie wasn't quite quick enough to banish from her eyes and his heart felt like granite inside his chest, a heavy leaden weight of black, bleak disillusionment.

'Maggie?' he pleaded rawly, when she continued to look at him in silence. 'I know you've got your city life, your city commitments...' He turned away from her a little, not wanting her to guess what he was thinking. She had told him about her business, her headhunting agency, and somehow he had managed not to betray to her his own feelings of distaste for the way of life she was reminding him of.

For a moment Maggie thought that he was just teasing her, that his suggestion was some kind of unfathomable male joke, but then she realised that he was actually serious. A fierce rush of emotion seized her—panic, fear, anger—forcing a deep chasm between her and her earlier feeling of love. In its place was a sense of betrayal, of disillusionment, a shocking and unwanted return from the idealistic world she had been creating in her own thoughts to one of reality.

'Me move in here? No, that's impossible,' she told Finn immediately, shaking her head as she pulled back from him. 'How could you possibly think—?' She stopped and looked round the kitchen and then back at him, unable to vocalise the full extent of her disbelief.

'Impossible?' Finn challenged her flatly. 'Why?' But of course he already knew the answer to his own question, just as he also knew that she was unlikely to give it to him, to be honest with him. His knowledge of her duplicity lay heavily against his heart. She had said that she loved him, but he himself had heard her call another man 'darling', with a note of soft tenderness in her voice that had said how much he meant to her.

He had hoped, prayed, that she might tell him about her lover, that she might say something, anything that would explain, excuse her lack of honesty, but she had said nothing, had given herself to him with a sweet hot passion that he had been totally unable to resist even whilst he had been despising himself for not being able to do so. For the first time in his life he had had to admit that he was unable to control his own feelings, unable to stop himself from loving her even whilst all the time knowing that she was committed to someone else.

When she had claimed to love him she'd been lying to him. When he had asked her to come and live with him she had refused—because of that someone else and the commitment she already shared with him. But she was obviously not prepared to tell him any of this. And if that made her a liar then what did it make him? What had he wanted her to tell him? That there was another man in her life but that because of what they had shared he now meant nothing to her whilst he, Finn, meant everything? Where the hell did he think he was living? Certainly not on planet earth. Cloud cuckoo-land was more like it.

A quick fling, a few days of sexual excitement with a stranger—that was all he was to her. He had known so many women like her in the old days, known them and felt sorry for them, for all that was missing from their lives, never imagining that one day he would fall in love with one of them.

Silently his stubborn heart begged her to confide in him, to justify its belief in her against the cynical contempt of his brain.

Maggie felt as though she was in shock. How could Finn possibly have imagined that she could live here? Angrily she blamed him for the destruction of her happy plans. And yet instead of exhibiting guilt, as he ought to be doing, something in Finn's manner was suggesting that he felt *she* was the one who was at fault. If he really loved her, as he had claimed to do, he would know instinctively how impossible it was for her to live somewhere like this.

The cold weight of his own disillusionment and pain lay like lead against Finn's heart, entombing it. Bitterness filled him, darkening his eyes and hardening his mouth in a curt line of contempt.

'You're right,' he agreed savagely. 'It is impossible.

What were you planning to do, Maggie? Just disappear without a word, without a Thank you for having me? I should have remembered, shouldn't I, that city women like you get a thrill out of indulging in a little bit of rough now and again—especially when it can be kept hidden away…walked away from? Well, perhaps before you do go I should really give you something to remember me by.'

Before Maggie could escape Finn moved, trapping her between the kitchen wall and his body and placing his hands on the wall either side of her as he deliberately lowered his mouth towards her own and began to kiss her with a savage passion that stripped away any veneer of polite social convention, revealing the raw, naked intensity of his anger—and his desire.

And hers she admitted bitterly as the sheer physical strength of her own need burned through her. Beneath his mouth she opened her own, taking angry biting kisses from his lips, her hands curling into small fists that clawed at the front of his shirt as she both clung to him and tried to force him away. The weight of his body as he lowered it against hers to imprison her made her want to fight against what he was doing and at the same time not merely to succumb to it but to feed it, until they were both consumed in the flames of their mutual hatred. She hated him and she wanted him. She wanted to destroy him and she wanted to wrap her body around him, draw him deep into it and keep him there, her prisoner, to do with as she willed, to make him helpless and dependent on her, to make him ache for her, need her, want her, to make—

The shock of Finn abruptly releasing her almost made her stumble, and that he should be the one to reject her made bitter passion burn in her eyes as they faced one another in silence.

It was Finn who broke that silence, speaking in a voice so empty of emotion that it caught at a vulnerable nerve ending she hadn't known she possessed, thickening her throat with tears of loss she would have died rather than let him see.

'I don't know which of us I despise the more.'

'I thought it was my sex that was supposed to be changeable,' Maggie responded, keeping her voice as light and indifferent as she could. 'This morning you swore you loved me, and now—'

'It wasn't love,' Finn interrupted her harshly. 'God knows just what it was, but it bore as much resemblance to love as the devil does to an angel.' Only he knew, thank God, just what it cost him to deny his feelings, to put pride and reality before the intensity and vulnerability of his love, the love he had now sworn to himself he must destroy.

Afraid of what she might, say, what she might betray if she allowed herself to speak, Maggie turned on her heel and left.

CHAPTER FOUR

MAGGIE hadn't realised that Shrewsbury was such a busy town. No, not a town, a city, she reminded herself, remembering her earlier phone call with her assistant Gayle. She had driven here in the hire car Gayle had organised for her and, having parked it, had set out to find the small designer shop Gayle had informed her the city possessed in order to buy herself some clothes. The city itself, though, had proved more distracting than she had expected. More than three-quarters enclosed by the loop in the river within which it was built, it possessed a strong sense of itself and its history.

It was here that the Welsh marauders had been held at bay, here too that the rich sheep farmers had brought their flocks. Maggie stopped, the bleakness of her own thoughts momentarily suspended as she caught sight of an entrancingly pretty courtyard down one of the city's medieval wynds. And then, as she turned the corner, she saw the shop she had been looking for, its windows as artfully temptingly dressed as any one of its London peers.

Pushing open the door, Maggie went inside, and a warmly smiling assistant came towards her. Giving her a quick shrewd look, Maggie recognised in the black suit she was wearing the cut of one of the fashion scene's most cherished designers. Quickly she explained what had happened and what she was looking for.

'I think we've got the very thing,' the assistant told her. 'It's a bit late in the season, but one of our regular clients, who is your size, cancelled part of her reserve order.' She gave Maggie a small smile. 'She met someone whilst she was working in New York and she's gone over there to be with him.'

Whilst she chatted she was moving through the clothes rails, deftly removing several items which she displayed for Maggie to examine. There was a mouth-watering honey-coloured full-length cashmere coat, butter-soft and blissfully warm, that Maggie fell immediately in love with even before she tried it on. When she did so, the gleam of approval in the assistant's eyes made Maggie wonder what Finn would think if he could see her in it—a weakness which she instantly tried to wall up behind a defensive barrier of sternly abrasive thoughts as she warned herself of the folly of allowing herself to think about him.

Why should she want to or need to anyway? Need to? The appalled expression that crossed her face as she slipped off the coat and handed it back to the assistant had the latter misguidedly assuming that it was caused by the cost of the coat, which she quickly explained was an exclusive designer model.

'It's fine. I love it,' Maggie assured her, and then winced at her own casual use of a word which had caused her so much anguish when it was applied to Finn.

Finn. Finn. Why on earth couldn't she stop thinking

about him? Why was she driven by this self-destructive urge to link everything she was doing with him? Maggie berated herself an hour later as she left the shop, wearing not just the cashmere coat but the suit she had bought as well.

For once a self-indulgent bout of retail therapy had failed to have its normal recuperative effect on her senses, and despite the warmth of the shop, and the restorative powers of the delicious cappuccino the assistant had produced for her, there was a cold emptiness inside Maggie, a feeling of misery and deprivation that reminded her unwantedly of the child she had once been, an outsider envying her peers who had all seemed to belong to happy loving families.

But that had been before she had gone to live permanently with her grandparents and become secure in their love, before she had taught herself that solitude and independence, both financial and emotional, were of far more value to her than an emotion which, like those who claimed to give it, could never be totally relied on. Now, back in the security of her own personal space, she couldn't understand why on earth she had behaved in the way she had And as for believing that she had fallen in love. She just didn't know how she could have thought such a thing. Love was far too unstable, untrustworthy and volatile to ever form part of her life-plan.

Firmly she congratulated herself on having come to her senses. What had happened was regrettable, and had revealed a previously unsuspected weakness within herself, but at least no lasting harm had been done. No doubt to Finn, undeniably good-looking and possessed of such sexual dynamism and power, she was simply another foolish woman who had made a fool of herself over him. Her face burned as she forced herself to remember just how much of a fool and how explicitly. Thank goodness she was never likely to see him again, she told herself as she checked her watch and hurried down the windswept street towards the car park where she had left her car.

It would only take her half an hour or so to drive back to the hotel in Lampton. She had arrived there the previous afternoon, dropped off by the taxi which had collected her from Finn's farmhouse. It had taken a considerable amount of patience and all of her many business skills before she had been able to persuade the manager of the hotel to lend her the money to pay her taxi fare—that and a telephone call to Gayle, who had not only vouched for her but also given the hotel manager her own credit card number to cover both the fare and a small cash loan to Maggie, to tide her over until the new cards Gayle had ordered for her arrived. Much to Maggie's relief, these had been delivered by hand to the hotel this morning.

Momentarily her footsteps faltered. She could still see and feel Finn's angry hostility towards her as he had watched her leave. Finn. What had happened between them had been an aberration, a totally inexplicable act completely contrary to her nature, and she was just thankful that reality had brought things to an end when it had.

Despite the warmth of her newly acquired cashmere coat Maggie gave a little shiver, so totally engrossed in her own thoughts that it was a handful of heart-stopping seconds before her brain registered what her body had already recognised: namely that the man standing in the middle of the street, as immobile as any statue, less than five metres away from her, was none other than Finn himself.

'Finn.' As she whispered his name Maggie could feel the physical reaction overwhelming her body, a cold drenching icy sense of shock as potentially dangerous as any floodwater could ever be, and an equally devastating blast of hot searing yearning as uncontrollable as a forest fire.

'Maggie!' Caught off guard, Finn felt the shock of seeing her crash through his defences. The urge to wrap her in his arms and carry her away somewhere private, where he could show her in all the ways that his rebellious body wanted to show her just what they could have together, was so strong that he had taken a step towards her before he realised what he was doing.

The sight of Finn striding purposefully towards her sent a wave of panic over Maggie. Immediately she looked for some means of escape. She just wasn't up to any kind of conversation with him right now, not with her emotions in such chaotic disarray. There was a narrow street to the side of her. Quickly she dived into it, her heart hammering against her ribs as she heard Finn calling out to her to wait.

After Maggie's departure from the farm Finn had told

himself that he was glad she had gone, reminding himself of all the reasons why a relationship between them could never work. But last night he had dreamed of her, ached for her, woken at six o'clock in the morning not just physically hungry for her but emotionally bereft without her—and furiously, bitterly contemptuous of himself for being so.

Finn could not possibly have known that she was in Shrewsbury; Maggie knew that. But nevertheless there was a sense of fatefulness in the fact that she had seen him, a sense of intensity that made her feel both frightened and angry, as though somehow she herself was to blame for his appearance, having conjured him up by her own thoughts. And even as she hurried away from him a certain part of her was feeling hectically excited at the thought that he might pursue her, catch up with her, and…

And what? Take her in his arms and swear that he was never going to let her go? Somehow magically turn back time so that…? Was she going completely mad? He was a farmer, not a wizard, she reminded herself sternly.

Ignoring the inner voice that warned him that nothing could be gained by prolonging his own agony, Finn made for the narrow lane Maggie had hurried down. But just as he was about to enter it he heard the familiar voice of his closest neighbour, an elderly farmer, who blocked Finn's access to the lane as he proceeded to complain to him about current farming conditions. Knowing that beneath the older man's complaints lay loneliness, Finn felt obliged to listen, even whilst he was inwardly cursing his appearance for preventing him from following Maggie.

What was she doing in Shrewsbury? Why hadn't she gone straight back to London? She had never told him exactly what it was that had brought her to Shropshire— they had been engrossed in discoveries about one another of a far more intimate and exciting nature than any mere mundane exchanges concerning their day-to-day lives.

Maggie... Finn closed his eyes as his ache for her throbbed through every single one of his senses.

As she reached out to unlock her car, Maggie gave a swift look over her shoulder. There was no sign of Finn anywhere in the car park. She told herself that she was glad he hadn't followed her. And if he had done she would naturally have told him that he was wasting his time. Wouldn't she? She started the car, then paused, giving the car park a final sweeping visual search before slowly driving away.

The auction wasn't due to take place until the following morning, but the agent for the sale of the estate had agreed to see her, and Maggie was still hoping that she might be able to persuade him to allow her to buy the Dower House before it went to auction. She was prepared to pay over and above its reserve price if necessary. She had to buy the house for her grandmother, who had sounded even more quietly unhappy than before when Maggie had rung her from the hotel.

Lambton was only small, a traditional country town with a mixture of various styles of architecture showing it had grown and developed over the centuries, and as she parked outside the agent's office Maggie realised that she could probably have walked there from the hotel faster than she had driven. Or at least in theory, she reflected with a rueful look down at the ravishingly pretty and impossibly high-heeled shoes she was wearing.

Finn would have taken one look at them and immediately rejected them as ridiculous and impractical—which no doubt meant that in his eyes at least she and the shoes were a good match.

Finn. Why on earth was she allowing herself to think about him—again? Had she forgotten already what he had said to her? Had she forgotten too that he had actually expected her to move into that remote farmhouse? A clever ruse, of course; he must have known that what he was suggesting was totally impossible, and would no doubt have been caught totally off guard if she had agreed. Still, from what she heard from her girlfriends, as being dumped went it had at least been original.

As she pushed open the door to the agent's office she had to battle against a dangerous feeling of loss that had somehow insidiously and unwarrantedly found its way into her thoughts, and she warned herself that she should be thinking about the reality of the situation instead of grieving for some foolish fantasy that she was very fortunate to have walked away from.

'I really am sorry,' Philip Crabtree, the agent, told Maggie ruefully, 'but we have strict instructions that the estate is to be auctioned and not sold prior to auction,'

'But why?' Maggie protested. 'Especially when I'm prepared to pay well over the reserve price.'

The agent sympathised with her. It was plain how important it was to her to acquire the Dower House, but as he had already explained there really was nothing he could do.

'I can't give you an answer to that other than to say that those are the instructions of the present owner.'

'Who is the present owner?' Maggie asked him—perhaps if she were to approach him or her direct she might be able to persuade them to sell outright to her.

'An American who unexpectedly inherited not just this estate but also a much larger one in another part of the country. He's been very specific about how he wants the sale to be handled. In fact originally he planned to attend the auction himself, but it seems that some unforeseen circumstances have cropped up that prevent him from doing so. I am sorry,' he commiserated when he saw Maggie's face. 'I can see how much you want the house.'

Maggie shook her head at his misconception. 'I don't want it for myself,' she told him. 'It's for my grandmother.' Briefly she explained her grandparents' connection with the property.

He was immediately even more sympathetic. 'I wish I could do more to help you,' he told her, 'but I have to follow our client's instructions. Perhaps I shouldn't tell you this, but we haven't had an awful lot of interest in the properties, so I don't think you need to worry about too much competition from other bidders.'

Thanking him for his time, Maggie made to leave. She knew she should have found his reassurances comforting, but she would far rather have preferred to know that the Dower House was going to be hers now rather than have to wait until after the auction.

Aspects of her life over which she was not in full control did not appeal to her one little bit, and besides…

As she hurried back to her car, huddled into her coat, she admitted reluctantly that she was anxious to leave Shropshire as quickly as she could—just in case. Just in case what? Just in case she should see Finn again, and he should have come to his senses and realised how wrong he had been; he'd tell her that he had had to find her to admit as much, declaring undying love for her, apologising to her and pleading with her to give him a second chance…

Just for a moment she allowed herself to dwell on this gratifying scenario—not because she wanted to see him again. No, of course not. No, it was simply a matter of knowing that she was in the right and feeling that he should concede as much. That was all. Nothing more. In fact so far as she was concerned it was actually a relief knowing that she was not going to see him again. Yes, quite definitely. Very definitely, in fact, she decided as she drove back to the hotel.

As she turned off the main road and into the long tree-lined drive that led to the Georgian mansion house of the estate, where the auction was to take place, Maggie reluctantly acknowledged the impressive grandeur of her surroundings. The trees were at the full height of their autumn glory, and the parkland stretching to either side of them was warmed by the morning sunshine. The house itself, which she could see ahead of her, was everything that was best about Georgian architecture, neither institutionally large, nor spoiled by any later unworthy additions.

She had a girlfriend in London, newly married and in her mid-thirties, who was desperate for just such a house—and desperate too, Maggie suspected, to remove her very wealthy and notoriously very susceptible new husband from the London scene and the attentions of other women. When Maggie had expressed her doubts about the wisdom of her friend turning her back on the successful career she had built up in the City, she had been told, smugly, that her friend had already made plans to work from the country, and that all she now needed to complete her happiness was the right house. And the right house apparently would have to be Georgian. Just like the one in front of her.

Undeniably it was beautiful, Maggie admitted as she parked her car at the end of a row of three other cars on the gravel forecourt to the house and got out.

The front door to the house was open, a notice there directing potential bidders to the room where the auction was to be held, and inside the hall on a dusty table was a pile of brochures the same as the one already in Maggie's possession, which listed the items to be auctioned.

The main house itself, along with its gardens, the farmland and estate buildings, were of no interest to Maggie—even if she had been able to afford them, which she most certainly could not. It would take a very, very wealthy person to be able to buy in full such an estate, she knew. No, her interest lay exclusively in the Dower House, which was listed as Lot 4 in the brochure, Lots 1, 2 and 3 being, respectively, the Georgian House she was now standing in, along with the stables and garages attached to it and its garden; the farmland; and the estate buildings which comprised barns and a pair of cottages. The Dower House was over a mile away from the main house, set in its own pretty garden and with its own private drive to the main road. Maggie could see as she walked into the large and once elegant, now slightly shabby drawing room, that Philip Crabtree had been correct when he had told her that there would be very few other bidders. Apart from the agent himself, and a young woman who was obviously working with him, there were only another six people in the room.

Gratifyingly, as soon as he saw her, Philip came hurrying over to greet her, introducing his assistant to her as he did so and explaining that the heavily built be-suited man standing studying the faded yellow silk covering the drawing room walls was a builder, and the man with him his accountant, and that he was hoping to buy the main house and the stables and garages for development purposes. The older man standing staring out of the window was, as Maggie had guessed for herself, a

farmer who wanted to buy the farmland, the younger
man with him being his son, and the young couple standing a little nervously side by side were hoping to bid
successfully for one of the cottages.

'Normally when we hold auctions in town we get a
lot of interested spectators who are there simply for the
entertainment value an auction provides, and if we'd
been auctioning off household goods we would undoubt-
edly have had far more people here, but the furniture,
such as it is, goes with the house, and is not of any
particular value.'

Philip stopped speaking and looked at his watch,
whilst Maggie waited. The auction was almost due to
start, and she could tell that the agent was slightly on
edge and preoccupied. Thanking him for the information
he had given her, she moved away.

The drawing room's yellow silk was faded where the
sun had touched it, and despite the existence of some
heavy old fashioned radiators the room felt cold and
smelled old and musty. Even so, to her own surprise,
Maggie found that something about it was giving her an
unfamiliar feeling of concern and compassion, almost as
though in some odd way the house itself was reaching
out to her, to tell her how much it wanted to be loved
and cherished and brought back to life.

Such unexpectedly intense and emotional thoughts
made her frown, engrossing her so much that it caught
her off guard to hear the agent announce that the auction
was about to begin.

As she went to join the small semicircle forming in front of him, Maggie was suddenly conscious of the way Philip was looking over her head and past her, as though…

Automatically she looked round, and then froze in disbelief as she saw Finn standing just inside the door. Her heart gave a fierce jolt and lurched against her ribs as emotions she couldn't control escaped from the captivity of her will-power. How had he found her? How had he known…? Fiercely she fought for self-control, sternly telling herself what she ought to be feeling and how she ought to be reacting, and it certainly wasn't with that dangerous mixture of sweetly painful anguish and joy she had now thankfully managed to subdue. How dared he seek her out like this? Here…now, when he knew she would be forced to acknowledge him. Yes, that was better. That was more the reaction she ought to be feeling.

But underneath her anger she could still feel all too keenly that sharp frisson of excitement and pleasure her body had given as it registered his presence. She wasn't going to speak to him now. He must wait until after the auction, until she was ready, prepared, her defences firmly in place…

'Ah, Finn, good. I was just beginning to think you weren't going to make it.'

The warmth and relief with which the agent was greeting Finn, the recognition his arrival produced, startled Maggie, putting a brake on her own thoughts. It was unpleasantly obvious that Philip had been expecting Finn to arrive—had been waiting for him to arrive, she recognised with sudden stark insight.

'Sorry I'm late,' Finn was apologising easily, switching his gaze from Maggie to the agent. But as soon as he had finished speaking to him he switched it back to her again, and any delusions she might have been foolish enough to entertain that he had come to the auction to see her would very quickly have been banished by the look of frowning wariness he was giving her, Maggie recognised.

The agent's assistant, obviously desperately anxious to make contact with Finn, all but knocked Maggie over as she hurried towards him, smiling up at him and standing so close that had she got any closer she would have been in actual bodily contact with him, Maggie reflected sourly as she monitored the other girl's openly awed and flirtatious manner.

And Finn, of course was enjoying every minute of her attention. What man wouldn't?

As she glowered at them both—a glower that was caused by distaste and her relief that she was far too in control of herself and had far too much self-respect to ever behave so needily to any man, Maggie quickly assured herself—Finn looked up and towards her, his gaze trapping hers before she had time to look away.

Just what was it she could see in those winter-blue eyes? Mockery, conceit, contempt, anger—all of those, plus a hostility and suspicion that infused her own gaze with a reciprocal hot resentment and pride. Yet, despite that, she still could not bring herself to drag her gaze from him, leaving it to him to be the one to end their fiercely silent visual engagement.

The auction had started, and Maggie concentrated determinedly on what was happening. The builder had started the bidding for the main house at a figure that made Maggie's eyes water a little, but her shock at realising the value of the property was nowhere near the shock she got when she saw the auctioneer looking past her and, unable to stop herself from turning round, realised that Finn was bidding for the house against the builder. Finn, a property-less farmer, bidding for a house which a nod of the builder's square-shaped head was already taking swiftly to the two million pound mark.

As the battle between Finn and the builder pushed the house up even further, Maggie could only look on in disbelief whilst Finn, a man whom she had assumed had to struggle financially, continued to bid for a property which was climbing inexorably towards three million.

At three and a quarter million the builder and his accountant exchanged looks, and Maggie saw the builder's mouth twist angrily as he conceded defeat.

As she battled with her disbelief Maggie saw the agent congratulate Finn with obvious pleasure before starting the bidding for the land.

Well, if Finn thought *she* was going to congratulate him he was going to be disappointed, Maggie told herself fiercely, and she deliberately turned her back on him. Surely he would leave now that he had got what he wanted? Her face grew hot as she remembered unwillingly her foolish assumption that he had come to the auction to seek out her. Thank goodness she hadn't said anything to him that might have betrayed that misconception—and her with it—to his scorn and rejection.

Finn watched grimly as Maggie turned her back on him. He was still battling with the sense of shock he had experienced on seeing her—and with the savagery of his unwanted pain when he had realised that she wasn't there, as his initial heart-wrenching belief had been, because of him.

Almost absently he nodded in the auctioneer's direction, signalling his interest in the land. It was entirely Maggie's fault that he had so nearly been late for the auction in the first place. A night of broken sleep interspersed with graphically emotional and physical dreams about her had resulted in him doing something he never did—oversleeping. Ever since he had first heard that this estate was coming up for auction he had been determined to buy it. Owning it would be the fulfilment of a decade long search. And yet now, instead of concentrating on the bidding, his thoughts were focused almost exclusively on Maggie.

What was she doing here? Bidding for one of the lots; that much was obvious from her intent concentration on the auctioneer and the sale brochure she was holding. But which lot? Not the main house, nor the land...

Finn frowned as he automatically raised his bid to meet that of Audley Slater. Audley was a local farmer whose family connection with the area went back over several generations. His land ran next to that of the estate, and Finn could well understand why he wanted to buy it, but Audley believed in intensive farming, and Finn knew that if he was successful he would drain the estate's water meadows, and probably sell the river's fishing rights. He wanted to retain the water meadows and if possible restore them to their original form.

No, Maggie couldn't be interested in the land—which left the cottages and the barns that went with them, and the Dower House.

Finn's frown deepened. Philip Crabtree, the agent, had been scrupulous about not discussing any other potential buyers with him, other than to say that both the Dower House and the cottages had attracted some interest. And, cautious about not revealing too much of his own plans, Finn had allowed Philip to believe that his bidding would be for the main house itself and the land.

Out of the corner of his eye Finn saw Audley Slater shaking his head as Finn raised his bid yet again.

Five minutes later, coming over to Finn after the auctioneer had finally signalled that Finn's bid for the land was successful, Audley told him bluntly, 'It will take one hell of a long time for you to make a profit out of the land at that price.'

Maggie could see Finn talking to the farmer he had just outbid. Next to her the young couple were huddled together, holding a whispered conversation.

'Not long now,' the agent told Maggie reassuringly as he walked past her.

The bidding for the cottages didn't take long. The moment the young couple realised that Finn was entering the bidding they virtually gave up. Maggie felt angry on their behalf as she saw their disappointment. Her stomach started to churn nervously as she heard the auctioneer announce the final lot for sale: The Dower House.

'This is a very pretty little Georgian house, with a good-sized garden, in an excellent situation, although in need of a certain amount of renovation and repair. I shall start the bidding at two hundred thousand pounds.'

Refusing to look at Finn, Maggie raised her brochure. 'Two hundred thousand,' she offered, hating the cracked anxious note she could hear in her own voice.

So Maggie was bidding for the Dower House. He should have guessed, Finn acknowledged bitterly. It would make a perfect 'weekend retreat' for Maggie and her partner—her lover. The lover she had denied to him existed; the lover he would never have known she possessed, given her sensual responsiveness to him, if he hadn't heard her himself on the telephone to him. He could just imagine what would happen if Maggie were to be successful in her bid to buy it. The house would be gutted. An expensive team of architects would be brought in to renovate the whole place, followed by equally expensive builders, and then no doubt one of the City's most trendy interior designers,

But the Dower House belonged rightfully to the estate, it was a part of its history, and there was no way Finn had ever intended to have city weekenders living right under his nose—any weekenders, but most definitely not

Maggie and her lover. Angrily he raised her bid. No matter how much it cost him there was no way he was going to have Maggie buy the Dower House. No way he could endure having her living there, no matter how infrequently, reminding him of certain things he had no wish whatsoever to be reminded of.

Maggie gritted her teeth and tried not to let her hostility show as she topped Finn's bid. He was doing this deliberately; she knew it. The auctioneer had virtually assured her that the Dower House was hers, that no one else was interested in bidding for it. She tensed as she heard Finn's clipped response to her bid. Three hundred thousand pounds—they had reached the house's reserve price, but there was no way she was going to stop now...

Oblivious to the interest the battle between them was now causing the others in the room, Finn and Maggie continued to outbid one another, taking the price of the Dower House higher and higher. Three hundred and fifty thousand, three hundred and seventy-five thousand, four hundred thousand...

When Maggie reacted sharply and fiercely to Finn's four hundred thousand with her own four hundred and twenty-five thousand, she could see the look of concern on the agent's face. The knowledge that he felt sorry for her, that he obviously felt she was getting out of her depth, only spurred her on. Four hundred and fifty thousand came and went, and four hundred and seventy-five. Maggie was way over her top limit now, but she no longer cared. All she cared about was winning... All she cared about was refusing to allow Finn to best her, to defeat her.

They were standing less than two metres apart and, unable to help herself, Maggie turned towards Finn.

'Why are you doing this?' she mouthed bitterly at him.

'Why do you think I'm doing it?' he mouthed equally bitterly back. 'There is no way I'm going to let you get the Dower House. No way, Maggie. No matter how much it costs me.'

No matter how much! The apprehension flooding Maggie almost overwhelmed her fury.

'Five hundred thousand pounds!'

A cold rush of icy shock rushed through Maggie as she heard Finn make his bid, his voice, like his demeanour, stern and unyielding. When he turned away from her to face the auctioneer an unfamiliar recklessness tore through her, totally obliterating the anxious voice of caution begging her to think about what she was doing. Instead of listening to it, Maggie started to make frantic mental calculations. She would have to remortgage her London flat, and borrow against the business as well as empty her savings accounts...

The reality of the financial ruin she could be facing if she allowed her pride its head finally got through to her, like a blast of cold air in an overheated room, making her shudder as she recognised her own danger.

She could sense the tension in the room, the sense of appalled fascination their duel was creating amongst the onlookers. Her pride urged her not to give in, but reality forced her to acknowledge that she could not continue. Her awareness of her own vulnerability tasted bitter, made her eyes sting with angry emotions she furiously refused to acknowledge. Holding her head high, she looked across at Finn properly, for the first time since the bidding had begun. Silently he looked back at her. His eyes were inimical and cold, his mouth a hard tight line of angry rejection

The auctioneer was waiting for her response to Finn's last bid. Reluctantly she shook her head, appalled by the unexpected and unwanted rush of hot tears choking her. Unable to face any more, she turned on her heel, heading for the exit.

She had just reached her car when Finn caught up with her. He had wanted to go to her before, but he had needed to speak with the young couple who he knew had been planning to bid for one of the cottages. He had learned that they were local youngsters, and that the young man had only recently left agricultural collage with excellent qualifications. It had immediately occurred to Finn that, since he would be in need of agricultural workers for the estate, he could both offer the young man a job and throw in the rental of the cottage at a suitably low rate, and he had wanted to make this offer to them before they left the house.

So far as Maggie and her desire to buy the Dower House went, he knew he had done the right thing, the only thing he could have done, but something about the way Maggie had looked at him as she conceded defeat had made him feel as though… As though what? As though he had behaved badly, unfairly?

'Maggie…'

The moment she heard his voice Maggie felt her emotions swamping her. Swinging round, her back against the door of her car, she glared at him. 'If you've come to crow over your victory, Finn, don't bother.' She gave a bitter laugh. 'I suppose I should have known that you would never allow me to win. How nice to be able to throw so much money away without counting the cost. I hope you consider it was worth it.'

'It was,' Finn assured her, suddenly equally angry, forgetting now, as he heard and felt her antagonism, the look of aching disappointment and pain he had seen in her eyes as she had acknowledged her inability to bid any higher. 'I would have paid twice as much to keep the likes of you from owning the Dower House, Maggie…'

'The likes of me?' Maggie was too incensed to conceal her feelings.

'City people. Weekenders,' Finn elucidated in a curt voice. 'The countryside should be for living in full time, not treated as some kind of manicured playground.'

'Oh, I see,' Maggie retaliated furiously. 'I'm good enough to take to bed, but apparently not good enough to have as a neighbour. Is that what you're trying to say? Well, for your information—' She stopped in disbelief as for the second time in less than half an hour the intensity of her emotions brought her dangerously close to tears.

'The fact that we went to bed together has nothing to do with the Dower House,' Finn denied—untruthfully. He could feel the tinge of colour creeping up under his skin as his conscience forced him to admit to himself that, contrary to his verbal claim, the fact that they had been lovers had everything to do with the fact that he didn't want her living in the Dower House. Not when he knew she would be sharing it—and her bed—with the man she had called 'darling', not when last night— all night, virtually—he had ached and longed for her, not when against everything he knew about himself a part of him still stubbornly refused to accept that there was no way there could ever be a proper relationship between them.

'You bid for the Dower House to spite me,' Maggie accused him once she had herself back under control.

'No,' Finn denied sharply. 'I had always intended to bid for the whole estate...'

'That's not what the agent told me,' Maggie argued, shaking her head. 'He told me that no one else was going to bid for the Dower House.'

'He may have believed that,' Finn acknowledged 'But—'

'But the moment you realised I wanted it you were determined that you were going to stop me,' Maggie cut in bitterly, too angry to conceal her feelings.

'There are other houses,' Finn pointed out.

'Not for me,' Maggie rejected grimly.

She looked white-faced and anguished, and ridiculously Finn found himself aching to comfort her. She had plainly replenished her wardrobe since she had left the farm. She was wearing the soft creamy cashmere coat he had seen her in in Shrewsbury, and a toning pair of trousers, with a fine knit top that clung to her breasts. She looked both elegant and expensive, and somehow softly vulnerable as well, the delicacy of her small heart-shaped face and huge brown eyes driving him to anger against himself for what he was feeling.

As she started to turn away from him a sudden fierce gust of wind caught at Maggie's unfastened coat, sending it swirling around her and virtually blinding her. As she reached to push it away so automatically did Finn. Their hands touched, Maggie's retracting as though it had been burned, leaving Finn's to somehow drop to her body, cupping her hipbone beneath the heavy folds of her coat.

Its fragility and the memories the feel of it evoked sent desire rocketing through Finn in a way that caught him completely off guard.

'Maggie.'

The urgency in his voice hit her senses with the same devastating impact as alcohol on an empty stomach. She could feel herself swaying in response to the desire she could hear running through that roughly urgent utterance of her name. She could almost see the images compressed in it. The two of them lying naked on his bed whilst he...

'Let go of me,' she demanded as she was deluged with panic—panic caused not by a fear of him but of herself and what she might do, what she might reveal if he continued to stay where he was.

But as she pulled back from him she realised there was nowhere for her to go, that she was already backed up against the car. Inside her she could feel her anger and excitement battling for supremacy. Finn was leaning towards her.

Her lips framed the word 'no' but it was too late. The kiss they exchanged was mutually hostile and denying, a fierce pressure of lips on lips, mouth on mouth, tongue battling with tongue as they fought to overcome one another and their own unwanted feelings.

If the time she had spent in Finn's arms had opened her eyes to the danger of her own susceptibility to his sensuality, then the kiss they were exchanging now was confirming just how right she had been to reject her feelings for him.

To feel such an intensity of emotion frightened her. To know that she was capable of wanting so passionately a man who made her feel so angry, of wanting him so intensely that a part of her was actually relishing the furious savagery of their intimacy, shocked and appalled her. And to know that she of all people was capable of being totally overwhelmed by emotions in a way that ran contrary to everything that was important to her filled her with a blind panic that somehow gave her the strength to wrench her mouth away from Finn's, to push him out of the way long enough for her to be able to pull open her car door and get inside.

As she drove off in a furious spray of gravel Finn

stared after her, fighting to regulate his breathing and his feelings. Where the hell had that come from? Absently he lifted his hand to his jaw, and then winced as his thumb pad brushed his bottom lip and found the place where Maggie had briefly savaged it with her teeth. He had never known such a passionate, contrary, downright dangerous woman—and he wished he didn't know her now.

Not when that woman was Maggie—and most definitely not when she was involved with another man.

CHAPTER FIVE

'I'M REALLY glad I managed to catch you before you left town,' Philip exclaimed as he came rushing into the foyer of the hotel just as Maggie was on the point of leaving. 'I'm really sorry about the Dower House,' he plunged on, ignoring Maggie's cool reception.

'You virtually told me that there were not going to be any other serious bidders for the property,' Maggie burst out, unable to keep her feelings to herself as she had promised herself she would do when she had first seen him hurrying towards her. After all, a humiliation like the one she had endured at Finn's hands was hardly something anyone would want to dwell on.

Unable to endure the thought of spending another night in Shropshire, she had decided to travel back to London immediately.

'I didn't think there were going to be,' the agent insisted.

He looked so anxious for her to believe him that Maggie knew he was telling the truth.

'Finn had told me that he intended to bid for the house, and the land, but I assumed that they were all that he was interested in. Like you, he asked me about the possibility of pre-empting the auction, but of course I told him that the owner was insistent on the property being broken up into lots and sold separately. We very often find a large house with land sells for more as separate lots, as indeed was the case. Finn has been looking to buy either a farm or a small estate locally for some time.' He paused and shrugged, looking uncomfortable as he told her, 'I really am sorry. I had no idea he intended to bid for the Dower House.'

Maggie gave him a thin smile. She suspected she knew exactly what had prompted Finn's unexpected decision to bid. The minute he had realised she wanted it he had obviously decided he was going to prevent her from getting it, no matter what it cost him.

Feigning a casual disregard she did not feel, she told the agent truthfully, 'Well, there was certainly no way I could have afforded to outbid him.'

Maybe not, but she had certainly tried hard enough, Phillip reflected inwardly. The Dower House had gone for more than twice its real market value.

Of course, he was very familiar with the red mist that could so easily overwhelm rival bidders, each determined to better the other, however, he could not remember ever experiencing such a charged atmosphere as the one generated by Finn and Maggie as they had fought for possession of the Dower House. It had been his concern for her ashen-faced despair as she had left that had prompted him to come in search of her, to assure her that he had had no prior knowledge of Finn's intentions.

'I know how much securing the Dower House meant to you,' Philip continued. There had been, he was sure, a sheen of tears in her eyes earlier as she had conceded defeat to Finn. 'Finn is a very generous man, something of a philanthropist. Perhaps if you were to approach him he might be prepared to rent the house to you... I know that he's offered to rent one of the cottages to Linda and Pete Hardy—they were at the auction. They're both over the moon and singing Finn's praises to whoever will listen to them, and now Pete is going to be working for Finn as well.' The agent chuckled. 'One of the reasons they had hoped to pick up the cottage cheaply was because whilst Linda works full time as a nurse, Pete didn't have a job.'

Even as she was digesting the agent's surprising news about Finn's generosity to the young couple who had wanted to bid for one of the cottages, Maggie's reaction to his suggestion that she throw herself on Finn's charity was as immediate as it was instinctive.

'No.'

Maggie could see that the harshness of her denial had shocked him. Forcing her lips to part in poor imitation of her normal smile, she told him in a less emotional voice, 'I wanted to give the house itself to my grandmother, not a rental agreement.'

She knew her excuse was not exactly logical, but there was no way she could tell the agent the real reason why she knew that Finn would refuse any request from her— for anything.

'Well, if you're sure, I'd better go and see Finn,' Philip was telling her a little awkwardly. 'Buying the estate is going to leave his bank account several million pounds lighter. Not that he can't afford it, of course.'

He was talking about Finn as though Maggie herself knew his circumstances, and even though she knew she would regret giving in to the temptation Maggie found it impossible not to say a little acerbically, 'I hadn't realised there was so much money in farming.'

The agent laughed. 'There isn't. And I'm afraid Finn's plans to extend the scope of his organic farming venture are not very popular with the likes of Audley Slater. But then of course Finn is not reliant on the land financially. He made a fortune as a City trader in the boom, and he had the foresight to take a large proportion of his bonuses in share options. He's worth millions,' he told Maggie.

Finn had been a city trader. Maggie fought to conceal her disbelief—she found it almost impossible to equate the man Finn had seemed to be with the stories she had heard about groups of wild young men who had become almost a byword for all types of excess. Things were different now, of course; there had been too many falls from grace for it to be otherwise.

The agent's revelation had affected her more deeply than she wanted to acknowledge, but somehow she managed to force a polite smile as he shook her hand before turning to leave.

Why hadn't Finn said anything? Told her—told her... Why had he let her think that the City was an alien concept to him? The certainty that she had known so little about him, been so wrong about his background, reinforced the fear she had fought so determinedly to subdue that with Finn, both he and their relationship would be outside her control.

The square was virtually empty as she hurried towards her car. What had she expected? To see Finn's Land Rover parked there? A dirty muddy old Land Rover! City traders drove up-market gleaming sports cars, the faster and more expensive the better. They dated models and actresses, and they loved city life and city women. But Finn did not. Finn felt only contempt for city women...

City women...or just one city woman...just her?

Sombrely Maggie got into her car. She had a long drive ahead of her, and the one thing she was determined she was not going to do was spend it thinking about Finn Gordon. Why should she? After all, he meant nothing to her. Nothing at all.

Finn didn't know why on earth he was bothering wasting his time like this. After all, he had far better things to do. And why should he apologise anyway? Grimly he crashed the Land Rover's gears, his attention more on his thoughts than what he was doing as he drove through the small town's narrow streets, heading for Maggie's hotel. Anyone would think he was looking for any excuse he could find just to see her And there was no way he was fool enough to do anything like that. She already had a man in her life, and even if she hadn't she had made it more than plain that she wasn't prepared to give up her city lifestyle.

Swinging into a convenient car park space, he reminded himself that he had had to come into the town anyway, to see Philip.

'Finn, I was just on my way back to the office to ring you.'

Cursing under his breath as Philip hailed him, Finn couldn't resist looking past him and across the square to the hotel. The memory of the angry kiss he and Maggie had exchanged outside the house still burned at danger heat...

'I'm just on my way back to the office now,' Philip was telling him. 'I've just been to see Maggie Russell— I felt I ought to. I hadn't realised that you were intending to bid for the Dower House, and I'm afraid I encouraged her to believe she had every chance of bidding success-fully for it herself. Luckily I just managed to catch her before she left.'

Left? Maggie had gone?

That wasn't some crazy desire to go after her that had him half turning back towards the parked Land Rover was it?

'I did suggest that she should ask if you would be willing to rent the house to her,' Philip continued, as Finn checked his reckless impulse. 'After all, from your point of view it would make much more sense to have it tenanted than left empty, especially with such a po-tentially good tenant—an elderly widow living on her own, and...'

'A what?'

All thoughts of going after Maggie gone, Finn stared

at the agent, the brusque sharpness of his voice causing the younger man to look confused.

'An elderly widow,' he repeated, persisting when Finn continued to look sternly at him, 'Maggie's grand-mother. Maggie told me the story when she came to my office to ask if she could buy the house prior to auction at the reserve price. I'm sure she won't mind me re-peating it to you.'

Finn had his doubts about that, but he quelled his conscience and gave Phillip an encouraging look.

'It seems that her grandparents lived in the Dower House as a young married couple. Maggie's grandfather has recently died, and she is concerned about the effect his loss is having on her grandmother. When she saw that the Dower House was coming up for auction she hoped that if she could buy it for her grandmother it might help to cheer her up a bit.'

Her grandmother. Maggie had wanted the house for her grandmother! Silently Finn digested the information Philip had given him. Equally silently he recalled Maggie's stricken look when she had realised that he was not going to allow her to outbid him.

The story the agent had told him was forcing him to see Maggie in a different light; to see her as someone who cared very deeply about those she loved. There had been no mention of her grandmother when she had told him about her successful business, but then there had been no mention of a lover either; in fact she had denied flatly that she had one.

Later that afternoon, as he drove back to the farm,

Finn discovered that he was still thinking about Maggie. As he drove across the ford he found he was actually looking down into the water, as though he might see one of her ridiculously impractical shoes there. He had noticed that she was wearing another pair of impossibly high-heeled shoes again today—only instead of seeing the choice of such footwear in the country and in such weather as gross folly, rather dangerously it had taken on an almost endearing quality, a special something that made her wholly and uniquely Maggie.

The fact that he had no close family of his own was something that Finn felt very keenly. His parents had married late in life, when their own parents had been elderly, so Finn had never known his grandparents. His father had died of a heart attack shortly after Finn's eighteenth birthday and his mother had died less than a year later. His own experiences had taught Finn how important family was. And as he drove into the farmyard he was deep in thought.

'And then Bas said that he didn't care how long it was going to take, he was going to keep on proposing until I gave in and agreed to marry him. So I thought I might as well save us both a lot of time and hassle and give in there and then.'

Politely Maggie joined in the others' laughter as they all listened to Lisa, drolly explaining how she came to be wearing a huge solitaire diamond engagement ring having sworn only weeks earlier that she was never ever going to get married.

The eight of them had been meeting up once a month for the last five years, all of them dedicated career women, all of them independent twenty to thirty-somethings, with their own flats, cars, accountants, and the wherewithal to buy their own diamond rings if they wanted them, and all of them determined to stay single. But gradually things had started to change.

Maggie wasn't sure she could pinpoint exactly how or when that change had started to happen. She just knew that it had, and from being earnest occasions on which they discussed their ambitions and successes over a meal at whichever of London's trendy eateries they were currently favouring, their get-togethers had begun to take on a much more personal note. The names of family members had begun to creep into their conversation, along with shamefaced confessions of parental or sibling pressure regarding their lack of partner and/or offspring, and a bonding at a much deeper level had come into being. Maggie had relished that closeness. Her friends were very important to her and she knew she wasn't alone in that feeling. Friends, as anyone who read a magazine or newspaper knew, were the new 'family'.

But now once again things were changing, and this time Maggie did not like it.

Caitlin had started it, returning from a holiday in Ireland to announce out of the blue that she was moving in with her boyfriend.

'My sister has this gorgeous baby,' was how she'd limply explained her change of heart, 'and I suddenly realised that I'm five years older than she is and that if I'm not careful...'

'It's your biological clock ticking away,' Lisa had told her knowledgeably, and that had been the start of it.

Now all of them had partners—all of them but her, Maggie realised as she listened to the others' laughter as they teased Lisa. But they were the ones who had changed, not her; just as they were the ones who sometimes looked a little self-conscious when they talked about their altered goals. As she talked to her friends right now, the unwelcome thought struck Maggie that it was almost as though Finn, with his back-to-nature, downshifting lifestyle, was more akin to them than she was herself. She felt...she felt almost as though she was an outsider, she recognised indignantly. And for some reason she was not prepared to analyse she felt like putting the blame for this on Finn's shoulders. And why shouldn't she? After all he was to blame for the fact that she was sitting here thinking about him.

'Of course Ma's jumped on the bandwagon now,' Lisa was telling them. 'I think I'm going to have to physically restrain her from organising a full-works wedding—and Bas isn't much help. He's virtually egging her on. Mind you, if he had his way there'd be no way I'd be decently fit to walk down the aisle. Waddle down perhaps; I've never known a man so desperate to become a father...'

'It's the new thing,' Charlotte interrupted. 'Men are baby-mad. Everywhere you look men are downscaling, cutting back their working hours, insisting that they want to spend more time with their families. I've lost count

of the number of couples I know who've moved out of
the City in the last year, and all of them because they
either have or want to start families.' She gave a small
shrug. 'And after all what could be more cosy than a
huge country house big enough for you to work from
home, and to house a family? Loads of people are trying
to persuade their parents to move in with them, too. I
mean, you just couldn't get any better childcare than
your own parents, could you?'

As Maggie listened to the heated debate that followed
she felt a cold sharp pang of alienness. But these were
her friends, women she had shared her hopes and dreams
with for the last five years—women who, after her
grandmother, formed her closest relationship circle.

'Well, moving out to the country is quite definitely a
hot new trend,' Tanya confirmed. 'I mean look at Greta
and Nigel. Of course those with the financial resources
to do so have always aimed to own a house in the country along with a city *pièd-a-terre*, but...'

As another heated flurry of exchanges broke out
Maggie remained silent, locked in the pain of her own
thoughts.

'You're quiet Maggie,' Charlotte noticed, turning to
look at her. But before Maggie could make any response
Lisa was laughing.

'Oh, Maggie thoroughly disapproves of us all. She
thinks we're traitoresses to the cause, don't you?'

'No, of course I don't,' Maggie denied, but she could
see that they didn't believe her. And she could see, too,

that suddenly she was excluded from their new shared closeness.

'Putting relationships first is the really happening thing now, Maggie,' Tanya told her gently.

Tanya worked in PR and knew all about 'happening' things. She had gone on holiday six months earlier—a tiny private island one could only visit by invitation—fallen in love with a fellow guest, and was now planning to give up her job and join him on his planned trek across the Andes.

Not that Maggie really needed anyone to underline for her what she already knew. She had lost count of the number of people she had 'relocated' recently who had insisted on 'time out for family' clauses being built into their contracts.

In the past their evenings out had ended late, but now it seemed everyone had things they needed to go on to—everyone but her, Maggie acknowledged. She could walk to her apartment from the wine bar where they had met. Halfway there she stopped outside a small super-market, and somehow or other she found she was walk-ing into it...

It was only when she was back outside that Maggie allowed herself to question just why she had found it necessary to buy the ingredients to make a chilli.

'Gran, why don't you come back to London with me? We could shop, and there's a wonderful new show we could go and see,' Maggie suggested to Arabella Russell that weekend.

'No...no. It's kind of you to think of me, Maggie, but I just don't feel in the mood. At least in this house I feel as though I'm still close to your grandfather, even though he was only here for a few short months.'

Her grandparents had moved into a smaller house six months before her grandfather's death, and Maggie could feel her throat aching with tears as she listened to her grandmother. In the few weeks since Maggie had last seen her she seemed to have become so frail. She looked frighteningly tired and defeated, as if...as though...

Thoughts Maggie dared not let herself form sent a sickening weave of panic through her. If Finn hadn't stopped her from buying the Dower House right now she could have been telling her grandmother that she had a special surprise for her. She could have been anticipating the pleasure and happiness in her eyes as she walked into the house she had known as a young wife. And Maggie just knew that in that house her grandmother would 'see' her grandfather as he had been when they had been young together, and that she would draw strength from their shared past happiness.

Finn... Finn...

She got up and hurried into her grandmother's kitchen, opening cupboard doors, searching...

'Maggie, what on earth are you doing?'

Guiltily Maggie looked round as her grandmother followed her into the kitchen.

'Umm...I was going to make some chilli.'

'What...?'

Red-faced, Maggie closed the cupboard doors. What on earth was happening to her? Why was it every time she thought about Finn she had this peculiar desire to make chilli?

Subliminal association was one thing; taking it to the ridiculous lengths of being physically compelled to make chilli just because the act of doing so brought her closer to her memories of the time she had spent at the farm with Finn was something else—and a very worrying and unwanted something else at that. Why on earth should she need to cling to those memories, as if…as if they were some sort of comfort blanket that she simply could not get through any anxiety without?

It was over a month since she had last seen Finn— well, five weeks, two days and seven and three-quarter hours, actually. Not that she was counting. Or cared. No, indeed not. Why should she? She didn't. No way. No way at all. She was perfectly happy as she was—more than happy. She was ecstatic. Her life was perfect…everything she had ever wanted it to be. At least it would have been if only her grandmother…

Damn Finn. Damn him and his ridiculous antagonism towards city people buying country property. What right did he have to dictate what others could and could not do? No right at all…other than the power that having far too much money gave him, to pay more than twice its value for a house just to stop another person owning it. Well, she just hoped he would be happy in his huge mansion, with his land and his alpaca and his empty Dower House… No, she didn't; she hoped he would be thoroughly miserable, because that was what he deserved. Unlike her beloved grandmother, who did not deserve to be unhappy at all.

Finn looked grimly at his surroundings. He had taken possession of the estate three days ago, his livestock had been moved to their new home, and he had successfully interviewed a first-class team of workers to help him put his plans into practice. So why wasn't he feeling more happy? Why, in fact, was he feeling distinctly unhappy?

From the library of the house, which was the room he intended to work from, he could see across the parkland to where the empty Dower House lay behind its high brick wall. Despite the warmth of the room—the house's ancient heating system had proved surprisingly efficient once it had been coaxed into life—the house had an air of chill emptiness about it.

According to Philip's assistant, it needed a woman's touch, and Finn knew exactly which woman's touch she had envisaged it having. But she wasn't his type. She was...not Maggie.

Angrily he dismissed the taunting voice whispering the words inside his head. He had been down to see the Dower House the previous day. Structurally it was sound and weather proof, but, like the main house, inside it needed modernising.

'Pity to let a place like this stand empty.' Shane Farrell, the man he had taken on as his gamekeeper, had commented. 'Wouldn't mind living here myself,' he had added hintingly.

'I'd planned to offer you the cottage next to Pete's,' Finn had told him, referring to the second of the pair of empty estate cottages he had bought at the auction. But Shane was right. It would be shameful to allow the Dower House to stand empty and deteriorate, especially when...

Walking back over to his desk, Finn picked up the telephone and searched the directory for the number of his solicitor.

The letter was waiting for Maggie when she arrived home at nine o'clock in the evening after a particularly trying day. Gayle was off work, ill with bronchitis, and the person Maggie had been discreetly courting on behalf of one of her best clients had telephoned her in a furious temper, from her home, to announce to Maggie that she had just been informed by her current employers that they knew what was going on—when she had specifically stressed to Maggie how vitally important it was that their discussions were kept a secret. Maggie suspected that it must have been the woman's partner who had leaked the information; they worked in the same field, but the partner was less well thought of. However, there was no way she could voice such a suspicion.

She had then had an equally irate call from her clients, who had been informed of what had happened by the woman herself. Appeasing them had made her late for lunch with another client—one who had a thing about punctuality. And then after lunch she had tried to ring her grandmother, and panicked when she had not been able to raise her either on the house phone or the mobile Maggie had insisted on giving her.

She had virtually been on the point of driving into Sussex to find out if she was all right when her grandmother had finally answered her mobile, explaining that she never liked to take it with her when she went to visit Maggie's grandfather's grave, which she did every week, because she felt that it was the wrong thing to do.

Without Gayle's capable hands controlling the day-to-day running of the office Maggie had found herself becoming bogged down in paperwork, and the last thing she had needed had been a long complaining telephone call from a man she had headhunted unsuccessfully the previous year and who had now decided that he had made the wrong move in electing to take a job competitive with the one she had been authorised to offer him. He had wanted her, in his own words, to 'fix things' so that he could accept her client's offer after all.

It was only sheer professionalism that had allowed her to grit her teeth and bite back her instinctive response to his patronising manner—that and the satisfaction it had given her to tell him sweetly that, unfortunately, 'fixing things' was quite simply beyond her capability.

Having opened her apartment door, she picked up her post before closing it again and then locking it. The block her apartment occupied was in a part of the City that had certain and specific restrictions on alterations to the elegant late-Georgian buildings, which meant that it was devoid of any kind of modern high-tech security features—much to Maggie's grandmother's relief.

'I'm sorry, Maggie, but I just don't trust those horrid little "speak into me" things—they never seem to be able to hear me properly,' she had complained, whilst Maggie had stifled her giggles. 'And I certainly feel much happier knowing that you are properly protected by a good old-fashioned doorman and that your apartment door has a proper kind of lock on it. Modern technology is all very well, but you just can't beat a real lock,' Arabella Russell had pronounced firmly. And Maggie had known better than to argue with her.

Whenever her grandmother visited Maggie's apartment she invariably brought a little 'home-made something' with her—not just for Maggie, who she was convinced did not eat properly, but also for Bill, the commissionaire, a widower who lived in a small apartment in the basement with a large ginger cat, and who seemed to conduct a running battle with the block's central heating and air-conditioning systems.

The arid heat of the central heating system felt stifling to Maggie after the cold outside, and just recently the apartment's silence had begun to grate a little on her nerves. She had even actually dreamed about waking up to birdsong and the sounds of the countryside.

Ridiculous, of course. She hated the countryside. It was dirty, and wet, and filled with impossible men wearing boots and driving battered old Land Rovers, masquerading as poor farmers whilst all the time owning squillions of pounds which they used to stop people like her from buying any of their wretched countryside.

Shrugging off her coat, Maggie started to open her

mail. And then stopped, dropping the letter she was reading in furious disbelief. What on earth...? How could...?
Angrily she walked into her small kitchen and then
walked back again, picking up the letter she had thrown
aside and rereading it.

Finn understood that she had wanted to buy the Dower
House for her grandmother, and on that understanding,
and on condition that she never at any time moved into
it herself with her lover, he was prepared to rent the
property to her at a favourable peppercorn annual rental,
to be agreed. If she would write back to him confirming
her agreement to these terms then he would instruct his
solicitor to begin the necessary legal proceedings and to
draw up a lease.

Maggie couldn't believe what she was reading. The
arrogance. To dare to...

Did he think she would actually...? And what did he
mean, on condition that she never at any time moved
into it herself with her lover? She did not have a lover.
How could he possibly think that when he...when she...
Oh, yes, now she could see the City trader coming out
in him. Of course to him the idea of sexual exclusivity
would be laughable.

Write back to him! Maggie was seething. Oh, no. She
had a far, far better idea than that!

CHAPTER SIX

As she drove west along the motorway Maggie was mentally rehearsing just what she intended to say to Finn. The 'time out' effect of a night to sleep on her fury had done nothing to lessen it. That he should dare to patronise her in such a way! And what had he hoped to gain from changing his mind? Her eternal grovelling gratitude? After that condition he had so insultingly outlined? Did he really think that if she had been involved with another man she would have behaved with him as she had, never mind allow him to dictate to her how, when or where she saw her lover?

Engrossed in her fury, she let the miles fly by, and it was only the sharp pangs of hunger gripping her stomach that reminded her how long it was since she had last eaten. Last night she had been too tired and then too furious to even contemplate eating. This morning she had been too busy thinking about what she intended to say to Finn and how she intended to make sure that he never made the mistake of trying to patronise her again to bother with any breakfast. A cup of coffee had been enough, but now her body was insisting that it needed nourishment!

Irritably Maggie drove more slowly, looking for somewhere to eat. It seemed a sensible idea to drive

straight into Shrewsbury rather than waste time driving
down country lanes, even it did mean a detour.

The smart wine bar where she eventually ended up
having her lunch reminded her very much of her City
haunts. As she waited for her meal to be served she
studied the eager group of young men and women seated
at a table close by. Absently eavesdropping on their conversation, she was forced to acknowledge that there was
very little difference other than that of location between
them and their London peers. She had even heard one
of the young men announcing that he had turned down
a move to London, though it would have meant a higher
income, because he didn't want to leave his friends or
his family.

Maggie gave a small shiver. Had Tanya been right
when she had teasingly claimed that Maggie was getting
out of touch, that she was clinging to values and beliefs
that were no longer viable? The girls had told her that
commitment with a capital 'C' was the new buzzword,
that it was generating an excitement, a sense of expectation and hope that everyone was eagerly reaching out
to.

'Deep down inside everyone wants to be loved,' Lisa
had claimed. 'It's just that our generation has had a hard
time getting round to admitting it. We were almost born
cynical. We looked at our parents and their lifestyles and
said, "No way, thanks. We'd rather be self-reliant and
single than risk what they put themselves through." But
now it's different—we're different. We can see where
they got it wrong and we can see how important and

valuable, how empowering the values they misguidedly thought unimportant actually are. Although naturally they do need a little fine tuning,' she had acknowledged without the slightest trace of any irony. 'And best of all,' she had added mischievously, 'it's men who are getting the commitment bug really badly this time round. Love, marriage, babies, families—that's where it is now, Maggie. The ''me'' generation and everything it represented is gone. Right now the big thing is the ''us factor''—sharing, caring, being. And I think it's wonderful.'

'I never realised your second name was Pollyanna,' had been Maggie's dry response, but deep down inside she had registered Lisa's comments—registered them and wanted to reject them because of the way they made her feel.

Unwilling to pursue her thoughts, Maggie paid for her lunch and left the wine bar. It would take her just over an hour to drive to the estate. The pithy observations she intended to make to Finn on his letter to her would not take very long to deliver and, since she had no intention of hanging around whilst he responded to them, she should be back on the road and on her way back to London before dark.

As she hurried to where she had parked her car she was aware of a sharp drop in temperature, and huddled protectively into her coat.

'I've searched all over London for that coat,' one of her friends had complained indignantly when she had seen her wearing it. 'There's a two-month waiting list for it. Where on earth did you get it?'

Smugly, Maggie had told her.

'Shrewsbury? Where on earth is that?' her friend had demanded.

As she left the cathedral city behind Maggie could see the grey-white clouds piling up slowly against the horizon. The countryside looked cold and bare, sheep huddling together motionlessly as she drove past them. At least Finn's alpaca should be used to winter weather with their heritage. Maggie started to smile as she remembered their cute small faces and huge dark eyes, their long necks weaving from side to side as they had watched her approach them curiously.

Was she going mad, grinning inanely to herself over the actions of farm animals? And worse still worrying about them?

This time she found her A road without any difficulty at all; indeed, she didn't even need to refer to her map in order to find the turn off for the Shopcutte estate.

The first thing she noticed as she turned into the drive was how much barer of leaves the trees now were; the second was that outside the house, right in front of the front door, she could see Finn's four-wheel drive.

That seriously stomach-churning feeling she was getting couldn't possibly be caused by doubts about the wisdom of what she was doing, by second thoughts, could it? No, of course not...

Of course not!

Even so, was it really necessary for her to spend so

much time carefully parking her car, reversing it so that it faced the drive—for a speedy and dignified exit—and then straightening it not once but three times until she was finally satisfied.

As a small confidence-booster she had only the previous week given in to the temptation to buy herself a pair of irresistibly delicious shoes, with high heels and peep toes—peep toes in winter: totally impractical—made in a deliciously soft tweed fabric. And she had even bought herself a matching bag. Not that she needed to boost her confidence in order to confront Finn...not at all. No, it had been entirely for other reasons that she had bought them. After all, she hadn't known then that she would be going to see him again. Had she?

The little designer dress she was wearing underneath her coat was equally impractical: a flimsy silk tea dress confection in fine voile printed with bees in which, the sales assistant had said, that she looked 'darling'. That comment had almost been enough to stop her from buying the dress, but in the end she hadn't been able to resist.

She had worn it to go and see her grandmother, who had exclaimed in delight that it reminded her of a dress she herself had worn in the forties. 'It was one of your grandfather's favourites...'

The little fake fur tippet that went with it somehow added to the dress's forties look, a look that was surely designed to be shown off in a sophisticated city setting, not worn in the depths of the country in the presence of a man who would only deride its impracticality—and who would no doubt lose no time in saying so.

Good, Maggie decided as she got out of the car and closed the door. She liked the idea of Finn giving her even more reason to take issue with him. Not that she had worn it to antagonise him.

Of course not.

As she left her car and walked towards the house she suddenly realised how still everything was, how silent. Not even the slightest breeze moved the air, which was winter-cold. The sky had a grey heaviness to it, and as she stared up at it a soft white flake of snow brushed her cheek.

Snow. In November. The end of November, admittedly, but it was still November. Wrapping her coat tightly around herself, she hurried up to the front door which, disconcertingly, immediately swung open.

'Finn!' she exclaimed in tones of angry resentment.

'Who else were you expecting?' Finn countered. 'After all, I do live here.'

As he spoke he stepped back so that she could walk into the hall—a much cleaner, brighter and better polished hall than she remembered from the auction, Maggie realised, as she took in the fire burning in the grate and the polished wooden floor, grateful that the need to inspect her surroundings was giving her time to prepare herself before she looked at Finn.

Not that she needed time or preparation. He was just a man, after all. Just a man who…As though he had grown tired of waiting for her to look at him, Finn moved into her line of vision, all six foot two, powerful muscle-packed maleness of him. Ridiculously, for such a cold day, he was wearing a thin white tee shirt, which hugged the contours of his chest almost as lovingly as the faded jeans he was wearing were clinging to his thighs.

Helplessly Maggie's gaze devoured him, her brown eyes smouldering passionately over every resented inch of him. How fatally easily she could picture him without that tee shirt, the soft whorls of his body hair flattened against the taut muscles of his stomach, just where she had stroked and then kissed the delicious hardness of the definition of his six-pack. Later, when he had growled and then groaned his appreciation and approval of what she was doing, she had moved lower, and then...

Dry-mouthed, she tried to wrench her gaze away from him and then realised as it clashed with his that he was studying her just as intently as she had been doing him. But it was derision and not desire she could see in his glance as it roved from the fashionably dark polish on her exposed toe nails, over her shoes, and upwards over her body, to rest momentarily on her face before dropping back to her feet.

This was better, Maggie acknowledged in relief as anticipatory antagonism filled her. Just let him say one word, make one criticism of her outfit and...

'Nice. It suits you.'

His calm words couldn't have had a more dramatic effect on Maggie. Stupefied, she stared at him, her mouth a round 'O' of bewilderment. Where were the contentious words of mockery and disapproval she had been expecting to hear?

As he watched her Finn wondered grimly if she had any idea just what the effect of seeing her was having on him, never mind seeing her wearing an outfit—a dress—which lovingly underscored every feminine centimetre of her. A dress she had no doubt bought and worn for her precious lover, Fin told himself, deliberately goading himself into jealousy and anger.

'Lucky, though, that the house's central heating system turned out to be working and efficient, otherwise I suspect you'd be rather cold. I'm using the library as my office. It's this way,' he told her, adding, 'I'm surprised you bothered to come all this way. Our solicitors could have sorted out the contract.'

Determinedly Maggie refused to move from where she was standing. 'There isn't going to be any contract,' she told him contentiously.

Finn turned and looked at her. 'No?'

His voice, like his eyes, was flat and hard, and awesomely polite in a way that sent a small shiver of electric triumph through her. He didn't like what she had said Good! Well, now he was about to hear something else he wasn't going to like.

Taking a deep breath, Maggie demanded, 'How dare you try to hold me to ransom? To tell me what I can and can't do and who with.'

'With whom,' Finn corrected her automatically.

Maggie took a deep breath, openly seething, but before she could speak, Finn continued calmly, 'Am I to take it that it's the condition that you will not be able to share a bed in the Dower House with your lover that's brought you…er…' He looked down at her shoes, before drawling tauntingly, 'Hot-foot down here.'

'My shoes, like who I share my bed with, are my concern, and only mine,' Maggie replied furiously.

'And, equally, who I choose to let the Dower House to and the conditions I choose to impose on that let are mine,' Finn countered grimly. 'Is having sex with him so much more important to you than your grandmother Maggie?'

It was like having a steel trap close round her mind. Something about him made it impossible for her to think logically and analytically, only to react emotionally, Maggie recognised as she denied furiously, 'No, it most certainly is not. My grandmother—' She stopped as her voice started to thicken with emotion. 'This has nothing to do with my feelings for my grandmother,' she insisted, almost hurling the words at Finn as she fought to avoid allowing him to verbally outwit her. 'This is about my right to live my life however I choose to live it, to share my bed with whoever I want—'

'And as we both know you are very good at doing that,' Finn intervened with a softly cruel emphasis that drove hot colour burning up over Maggie's skin. 'Very, very good,' Finn emphasised deliberately.

Maggie had started to clench her hands into small tense fists.

'I am perfectly prepared to allow you to rent the Dower House for your grandmother's occupation—

Philip explained her circumstances to me,' Finn continued.

'He had no right to discuss my private business with you—' Maggie began, but once again Finn stopped her.

'You should be grateful to him,' he told her challengingly. 'He was, in a manner of speaking, defending you, insisting that you did not want the Dower House as a pretty country toy you could retreat to with your lover, but for far more altruistic reasons.'

'You told him that I have a lover?' Maggie demanded hotly. Her grandmother was old-fashioned; if she were to live at the Dower House and hear gossip that her beloved granddaughter had a lover—and, moreover, a lover she knew nothing about—she would not just be shocked, she would be hurt that Maggie hadn't confided in her herself, Maggie knew. 'How dare you?' she continued furiously. 'How dare you lie about me like that—?'

'Lie?' Finn cut her short, tightlipped now as anger glittered dangerously in his eyes. 'Me? I heard you myself on the phone to him at the farmhouse. ''Darling…''' he whispered, savagely mimicking Maggie's softly husky voice.

Baffled, Maggie stared at him. 'The only people I telephoned from the farm were my assistant and my grandmother…' Her voice faltered, and then grew stronger as she repeated, 'My grandmother…my beloved, darling, grandmother.'

Finn went completely still. There was no mistaking the sincerity in her voice. And no mistaking her fury either. Perhaps there was more of the City trader left in him than he had thought, he admitted wryly, as he shrugged his shoulders and prepared to unashamedly blag his way out of the situation.

'So I made a mistake.'

A mistake! Maggie's chest heaved, sending the bumble bees into delicious activity—to Finn's male eyes at least. Her eyes flashed, and he could have sworn she grew two inches taller as she confronted him.

'You blacken my reputation; force me out of the bidding for the Dower House, send me the most repellent letter I have ever received, try to tell me how I should live my life, correct my grammar—and you call it a mistake.'

Fresh activity amongst the bumble bees held Finn's glance awed and enthralled, but thankfully Maggie herself was far too wrapped up in her own anger to notice his inability to drag his attention from her breasts—breasts which, as he already had good reason to know, felt and tasted every bit as deliciously feminine and honey-sweet as they looked.

Later he might admit to himself that perhaps what followed was an extremely contentious piece of verbal baiting on his part, but at the time...

'Haven't you forgotten something in that list of supposed crimes?'

The mild tone of Finn's voice caught Maggie offguard. For some reason she couldn't fathom, and didn't dare to try to over-analyse, the sight of the muscles in his bare arms, when he folded them across his chest before leaning back against the wall, sent a soft little shiver of sensation all the way through her body, causing her to curl her toes slightly. There was something sexily awesome about Finn's arms, something about their strength, their power to hold and protect, something about their gentleness when he had wrapped them around her, something that right now was making her want...

Shakily she forced herself to concentrate on what Finn was saying—something about a crime she'd forgotten. But before she could phrase any question Finn was answering it for her, telling her succinctly and, she was sure, with a great deal of enjoyment, 'Going to bed with you.'

Going to bed with her? Was that how Finn saw what had happened between them? As a crime? Maggie didn't like the sharp pain that seared her: a pain which she was determined to ignore. Well, if it was she was just going to have to make sure he knew that, as far as she was concerned, their lovemaking—no, their *sex*, which after all was the correct word for it—had meant nothing at all to her!

Feigning uninterest, she shrugged and looked away from him. Lying to him was one thing; lying to him when he had that penetrating gaze of his fixed on her was very definitely another. 'I'm an adult. I can go to bed with whoever I like.'

'Like?' Finn pounced with lethal speed.

Hot-cheeked, Maggie tried to brave it out. 'Neither of us has ever denied that the sex between us was good.'

Finn tightened his folded arms, not trusting himself to move. If he did, if he got within range of her, she would be right there in those arms, whilst he...

'Anyway, I haven't come here to talk about sex,' Maggie told him, furiously aware of her own red face and the decidedly dangerous male gleam now lighting Finn's eyes.

'No, talking about it is a complete waste of time,' Finn agreed, straight-faced, 'especially when—'

Had she any idea how adorable she looked: all furious embarrassment, all desirable woman, the only woman he...

'I came to talk to you about your letter,' Maggie told him sharply. 'How dare you patronise me by offering me the Dower House at a peppercorn rent? I don't need your charity, Finn. I can afford to pay my own way through life. And—'

'I wasn't doing it for you. I was doing it for your grandmother,' Finn told her, completely silencing her. 'You may be able to afford to pay any amount of rent, but I suspect things may be different for your grandmother.' He held up his hand when Maggie would have interrupted him. 'Yes, I know that you'd pay the rent for her, but if she's anything like most other members of her generation—and I suspect she is—after all her granddaughter has to have got her determined independence from somewhere—she will want to pay the rent herself.'

Maggie knew that he was right. A huge lump of mixed pain and guilt was filling her throat, making it impossible for her to speak. How it was that Finn had found a flaw in her plans that had escaped her? How was it that he had somehow known exactly how her grandmother would feel when she herself had not?

Maggie wasn't sure which she resented having to acknowledge the more: his unexpected sensitivity towards the feelings of an elderly woman he didn't even know, or the fact that that sensitivity made her feel guilty because she herself had not recognised the need for it. Her grandmother was her grandmother, not his.

'I can find my grandmother another house,' she told him challengingly.

Finn gave her a hooded, unreadable look that for some reason made her heart bounce around inside her chest like a rubber ball.

'Yes, I'm sure that you can. But as I understood the situation the reason you wanted the Dower House for her was because of your grandparents' past association with it. Of course, no doubt, during the course of a long marriage they would have shared other homes together...' He paused, and Maggie looked angrily away from him.

'They began their married lives together in the Dower House,' she found herself admitting reluctantly.

As he surveyed her averted profile Finn felt a dangerous thread of unwanted tenderness for her curl itself sinuously around his heart. He itched to take hold of her and shake her for her stubbornness, and at the same time he ached to hold her, to banish from her eyes and her voice the pain he could see and hear in them. 'You were very close to both your grandparents?' he guessed.

Maggie couldn't deny it. 'Very,' she agreed shortly, and then to her own consternation she heard herself telling him unsteadily, 'They gave me a home, security, love, when my own parents—' She stopped and shook her head, her mouth compressing, her expression betraying how much she regretted saying as much as she had.

But Finn ignored the invisible 'keep out' signs she was posting and pressed on ruthlessly. She intrigued him, baffled him, infuriated him, and made him ache with the intensity of those emotions. He was determined to find out just what it was that made her tick, what it was that made her so antagonistic towards him. 'When your own parents what?' he asked her.

Maggie closed her eyes. This was a conversation she wished she had never begun. She never talked about her parents to anyone. Not even her girlfriends knew how frightened, how insecure, how unwanted the careless, casual attitude of her mother and her father had made her feel.

She could still see the look of irritation on her mother's face when she had begged her to attend her school play.

'Oh, darling, no. James is taking me out to dinner tonight, and anyway you wouldn't really want me to be there, would you? You know how bored I would be...'

Oh, yes, Maggie had known how bored she would be, how bored she so often was with Maggie herself.

'Nothing,' Maggie denied fiercely in answer to Finn's question.

As she turned away from him, because she didn't want Finn to see her expression, she wasn't prepared for the sudden movement he made as he levered his body away from the wall and strode towards her, grasping her shoulders with his hands before she could escape.

'They hurt you didn't they, Maggie?' he guessed. 'They—'

'No.' Maggie hurled the denial at him like a thunderbolt, but she could hear in her voice, as clearly as she knew he must be able to himself, the fear and anguish that made a mockery of her lie.

'Maggie…'

'I don't want to talk about it. It isn't any of your business anyway. My parents were no different from countless other people of their generation, believing that they had a right to put themselves and their own happiness first. Their mistake was in having a child like me, who wanted…'

To her own horror Maggie could feel her eyes filling with tears. Frantically she tried to wrench herself out of Finn's grasp, lifting her gaze furiously to his and then stiffening as she saw the compassion in his eyes.

Every ounce of her tensed body shrieked a silent scream of outrage that Finn could almost hear as he recognised how furiously she was rejecting his pity for the child she must have been.

'No, Maggie,' he corrected her gently. 'Their mistake was in not valuing the gift they had been given. '

Something about the dark warmth of his voice was compelling her to look at him, to relax into him, to lift her face towards his and...

As he looked down into the cloudy emotion of her brown eyes Finn knew that he was lost. His gaze skimmed her face, her mouth. Her mouth...

Maggie could feel the soft groan he gave vibrating through his body. Feel it? What on earth was she doing standing so close to him? Frantically she pulled away from him, her eyes brilliant with tiny shards of anger.

'I've had enough of this,' she told him furiously. 'I'm leaving—now.'

Quickly she spun round on her heel, heading for the front door.

'Admirable exit line though that was, I'm afraid that you aren't going to be able to go anywhere,' Finn told her dryly.

Not leave? He wasn't going to let her leave? Anger battled against fiercely sensual pleasure and excitement—and lost.

'What do you mean?' Maggie made herself challenge him. What was she going to do if he absolutely refused to let her go, if he insisted on keeping her here with him? A shocking thrill ripped through her, heating her face—and her body—with dangerously inflammatory secret thoughts and memories.

'Take a look outside,' Finn invited her, going to open the front door.

Whilst they had been arguing the afternoon had darkened into dusk, but it wasn't the darkness that made

Maggie gasp in disbelief as she stared out of the open door, her chagrin that he hadn't, after all, been speaking out of a desire to keep her with him obliterated by the sight that greeted her disbelieving gaze. Whilst they had been arguing dusk wasn't the only thing that had fallen. Everything was covered in a thick blanket of snow—snow that was still falling, driven by a strong and very cold wind, so that in the corners of the building it was already forming peaked drifts. The side of her car was a mask of white, only the double row of trees marking where the drive lay.

Maggie gulped and looked at Finn.

'It probably looks worse than it is. Once I get to the main road…'

'No way,' Finn told her, shaking his head. 'They were giving out blizzard warnings earlier, urging people not to travel. These country roads—even the A roads,' he added dryly, 'are subject to heavy drifting. I'd have second thoughts about driving in this in the Land Rover, and there's no way I'm going to let you take the risk of going out in it.'

'There were blizzard warnings?' Maggie demanded, glowering at him. 'Why on earth didn't you say something…tell me?'

That was a question Finn had been asking himself from the moment he had seen her arrive. And one he had still found no satisfactory answer to—at least not one which would satisfy any logical criteria! 'You didn't give me much chance,' he pointed out. 'You were determined to say your piece, and…'

Maggie shook her head in disbelief. 'Now what am I going to do?'

'There's only one thing you can do,' Finn told her. 'You'll have to spend the night here.'

Maggie gritted her teeth against her ire and exasperation.

'What kind of county is this?' she demanded irritably. Its extraordinarily changeable weather conditions had to be peculiar to the area; there had certainly been nothing on her car radio as she had driven west to warn her of impending blizzard conditions! Impassable fords, snow in November. 'That's twice now we've been marooned together. You'd never get anything like this happening in London,' she told Finn irritably as she surveyed the inhospitable not to say downright dangerous arctic scene in front of her.

As the wind twisted blowing an icy sheet of snow over her she stepped back into the warmth of the house. Already her face and hands were stinging from the cold.

'What about the alpaca?' she asked Finn anxiously. 'Will they be all right?'

Finn busied himself closing the door before answering her. He didn't want her to guess that he was smiling. 'The alpaca will be fine,' he assured her, keeping his face as straight as he could. 'They're used to the cold.'

'But the little ones? The babies?' Maggie protested, remembering the young animals she had seen with their mothers.

'They'll be fine,' Finn repeated.

She was looking at the closed door almost as though

she was going to rush through it and check on the animals herself, which might prove rather embarrassing, seeing as they were all tucked up safely in a specially enclosed field complete with protective bales of hay and an open barn to go into for shelter. He and Shane had moved them there only this morning, after hearing the weather forecast. The same forecast he had omitted to mention to Maggie!

'In your grandmother's time there would have been deer in the park,' he told Maggie, intending to distract her. 'I'm looking forward to meeting her. She must know quite a lot about the recent history of the house if she lived here. The two sons of the family who would have owned it at that time were both killed during the War, and the estate then passed to a second cousin who already owned a much larger estate in Scotland.'

'What do you mean, you're looking forward to meeting my grandmother?' Maggie interrupted him ominously. 'I've already told you, she won't be coming here.'

There was a long pause before Finn asked her with deliberate emphasis, 'Are you really prepared to do that, Maggie? Let me ask you something. If it were anyone else but me offering you a lease on the Dower House would you refuse it?'

Maggie bit her lip.

'I don't want to discuss the subject any longer,' she told him sharply, adding in a very formal and grand voice, 'If you would just direct me to my room?' Pointedly she lifted her eyebrows and looked at Finn.

'Your room. Mmm... Unfortunately, there's a slight problem. As yet there is only one functional bedroom...'

'One bedroom?' Maggie repeated warily.

Soft brown eyes clashed with winter-blue.

'One bedroom,' Finn agreed softly.

CHAPTER SEVEN

ONE bedroom!

And they had spent what was left of the fast-fading daylight arguing about which of them was going to occupy it—or rather which of them was going to make the noble gesture of sleeping in the drawing room on one of its two sofas.

In the end Finn had won, but only because she had allowed him to, Maggie defended her own capitulation mentally. Only because he had thrown down a trump card by declaring, 'Since this is my home, I rather think that the decision of who sleeps where lies rather more in my hands than yours, Maggie. And, as your host, I fully intend to claim the right of giving up my bed for my guest.'

Maggie had clenched her teeth together at those words 'host' and 'guest', but in the end she had had to give in. And now here she was, standing in Finn's bedroom, staring out of the window into the starlit snow-covered landscape. Turning her back on it, she faced the bed. Something she had deliberately been avoiding doing since Finn had shown her up here half an hour ago, suggesting that she 'make herself at home' whilst he cooked them a meal.

It was, as she might have expected given the size of

the room—and Finn himself—very large. Very large. Large enough not just for two adults but potentially large enough for a handful of children as well. Children! Now, where had that thought come from? And, far more disconcertingly, why?

Concentrate on the room as it is, Maggie warned herself. Instead of fantasising about…about things there is totally no point whatsoever in even thinking about—or even wanting to think about!

Its high ceiling and decorative plasterwork were typical of the period of the house, and someone—Finn— had washed the walls in a fresh covering of subtly tinted bluey-green paint, picking out the plasterwork in white and a denser colour of the tint. But, whilst Maggie would normally have thoroughly approved of the plain white bedding and bare stripped floorboards, somehow the room cried out for something softer and warmer.

That floor would be so cold on those little bare feet as their owners came rushing into their parents' room to join them in bed, and one would have little inclination to linger for long intimate embraces en route from bathroom to bed, surely, without the softness of a thick carpet to curl one's toes into. No, what this room needed was the sensually rich fabrics that its original builder must have favoured, and furniture, too: the kind of furniture owned by her grandmother, furniture one polished with traditional beeswax and lavender polish.

Maggie gave a faint sigh and then blinked. Just for one suffocating second, whilst she had been looking absently at the bed, she had somehow or other seen Finn lying there, propped up against the pillows, his body bare, lean, muscular and oh, so inviting, his hair ruffled from sleep, his jaw malely rough, his mouth curling invitingly as he looked at her...

Quickly Maggie blinked again, banishing the wickedly tantalising image. In the room's *en suite* bathroom she tidied herself up, and placed the clean warm towels Finn had taken from the airing cupboard and given to her on a stool. The huge towelling robe he had given her, which was patently one of his, she determinedly placed at the bottom of the pile.

It was time she went back downstairs. If she didn't Finn might actually start thinking that she wanted him to come looking for her. As she hurried to the bedroom door she glanced towards the window, her forehead furrowing in a darkly accusing frown. It had started to snow again. It was almost as though the weather was determined to cause her problems, to keep her here with Finn.

'We'll have to eat in here,' Finn announced as Maggie walked into the kitchen. 'I suppose ultimately I'm going to have to get designers in to revamp the place, but at the moment—'

'Why didn't you tell me that you used to work in the City?'

The abruptness of her unplanned question made Maggie wish she hadn't asked. The high standards and professionalism she normally demanded of herself made her blush with embarrassment at her own unfamiliar gaucheness, but to her relief, instead of reacting with a cool put-down, Finn looked at her searchingly for a few seconds before replying quietly, 'It's a part of my life I've put behind me and which has no real relevance to the way I live now other than that the money I made then has made it possible for me to choose my own future.'

'You can't say that,' Maggie objected immediately. 'Everything that happens in a person's life has relevance.'

'You mean like your own relationship with your parents?' Finn countered.

Brown eyes met blue, the pride and pain in the brown an immediate barrier to the challenging masked compassion in blue.

'Whatever unhappiness I experienced through my parents' lack of love for me was more than outweighed by the love of my grandparents,' Maggie defended herself sharply. 'You, on the other hand, are obviously hanging on to your bad feelings about city life and city people.'

She had a very quick and incisive mind, Finn acknowledged with reluctant admiration, If there was one thing he did miss about city living in his current solitary life, it was the buzz that the exchange of conversation, opinions, news and views with other like-minded people had given him.

'Not really,' he denied, giving a small shrug as he told her, 'It's simply that I've moved on inwardly, as well as physically, and the man I am now wants a hell of a lot more out of life than material success. And besides...' He paused, opening the oven door to study its contents before adding sombrely, with just enough contempt in his voice to make Maggie's face sting with angry resentment, 'I've seen too many people damaged or destroyed by the pursuit of wealth and success—driven to abuse themselves and others by their fear of what they consider to be failure—to have any illusions left.'

'It isn't city living that causes that,' Maggie protested.

'Maybe not, but it doesn't help. The lasagne is just about ready,' he informed Maggie. 'And, since they say that arguing is not conducive to good digestion, I suggest that we find something else to talk about.'

'I've got an even better idea,' Maggie told him acerbically, adding without waiting for his response, 'Why don't we just eat in silence?'

'A silent woman! Is there such a thing?' Finn mocked her as he removed the lasagne from the oven.

Maggie threw him a murderous look, but somehow managed to restrain herself from making any verbal response.

Half an hour later, her stomach deliciously full, her earlier antagonism and with it her mental vow to herself momentarily forgotten, Maggie announced, 'That was good. I hadn't realised how hungry I was.' She stopped abruptly as she realised what she had done, but instead of taunting her for breaking her self-imposed silence, Finn simply looked at her.

When she forgot to be on her guard against him there was an endearing sweetness about her which gripped him by the throat and the heart. And wasn't his body well and truly reacting to that knowledge, and to her?

He could feel his glance sliding dangerously towards her mouth, the appetite he wanted to satisfy having nothing whatsoever to do with food, and he hastily dragged it back before Maggie could see.

If he had thought the buzz he had once got from the City traders' always-on-the-edge lifestyle possessed too much dangerous and addictive excitement, it was nothing to the charge this reckless game of advance and retreat he and Maggie were now putting one another through. But, despite what common sense and caution were telling him, he still couldn't resist the opportunity presenting itself to him.

'A city woman who likes to eat. Now you *have* surprised me. Although I suppose I shouldn't be surprised, after all...' There was a gleam in his eyes when he paused that made Maggie's muscles tense as she waited for the blow she knew was about to fall. But when it came it was not what she had been expecting, and its effect was so devastating that she suspected her reaction must have given her away completely. 'After all,' Finn continued in a softly sensual voice that felt like male fingers stroking her skin, 'They do say that a woman with a healthy appetite for sex has a healthy appetite for all the pleasures of life. Another glass of wine?' he offered, indicating the bottle of red wine he had opened when they had begun their meal.

'*No!* No, thank you,' Maggie amended in a calmer voice as she battled against her reaction to his soft words.

A healthy appetite for sex. Did he have to remind her…to torment her…?

'Perhaps it's stopped snowing. Perhaps I can leave after all.' Maggie knew that she was gabbling, giving away her panic, and her movements were flustered as she started to stand up and then sat down again very quickly as Finn moved towards her and reached out for her empty dinner plate. If she stood up now she would be standing right next to him. Just the thought of that happening was enough to make her whole body quiver as tiny rushes of nervous excitement darted through her. Agitatedly she picked up her wine glass and drank from it. She knew that Finn was watching her, and that was making her feel even more nervous.

'It hasn't,' Finn responded grimly. 'You can't. And even if you could, after three glasses of wine I doubt you'd be legally able to drive.'

Three glasses? Maggie was horrified. Had she really drunk so much? A glance at the glass in front of her was enough to have her saying with solemn dignity, 'I've only had two and a half.'

'That's still over the legal limit,' Finn told her. 'And besides,' he added, 'in those ridiculous shoes you're wearing you couldn't make it through one centimetre of snow, never mind closer to ten.'

'Ten? No, that's impossible,' Maggie gasped, adding with a glower, 'And will you please stop criticising my shoes? Just because you don't like them.'

Finn, who had been loading the dishwasher, turned round, subjecting her to the full heart-rocking force of a look of such intense sensuality that it literally made her moan softly out loud.

'I never said anything about not liking them,' he told her succinctly. 'Simply that they were impractical.'

'"Ridiculous" was the word you used. Not impractical,' Maggie reminded him. She felt as though she were clinging helplessly to a very precarious rock in the middle of an extremely dangerous body of water. Pushing back her chair, she stood up. 'I'm tired...I think I'll go to bed. Hopefully the snow will be gone by morning, and I'll be able to make an early start.'

Why on earth was the way Finn was looking at her making her stammer and walk away from him so self-consciously, all too aware of the way the height of her shoe-heels was making her body move?

As though he had read her mind, when she reached the door she heard Finn saying softly, 'I was wrong. Neither ridiculous nor impractical is the right description for them. But provocative—now, that *is*.'

Provocative! If Finn was trying to imply that that was what she was, then...

But for some reason, instead of turning round to confront him and demand a retraction of his statement—a statement that could quite definitely be described itself as both ridiculous and provocative—Maggie discovered that she was actually hurrying away from him...running away from him? From him or from what he was making her feel?

In the silence of his now Maggie-free kitchen, Finn wondered irritably what subtle ingredient her perfume possessed that made its delicate fragrance linger so long. He could swear that his bedroom at the farm had continued to carry her scent right up until the day he had moved, and now here she was occupying his bedroom yet again...his bedroom...his bed...his life...his heart...

Grimly he closed the door of the dishwasher and switched it on, glancing out into the snow-covered yard beyond the window as he did so. Snow in November? It was unseasonable, unsettling and should have been unfeasible—like his feelings for Maggie?

Maggie woke up with a start, wondering at first, in the semi-darkness of the unfamiliar bedroom, illuminated by the bedside lamp she had deliberately left on, just where she was. And then she remembered. She was in Finn's house, in Finn's bed. Finn.

Her mouth felt dry from the wine she had drunk. She was desperate for a glass of cold water. Hesitantly she sat up. It was just gone midnight. Pushing the bedclothes aside, she got out of bed. When she opened the bedroom door she saw that the landing and stairs were in darkness. A sharp nervous frisson shivered through her. Loath though she was to admit it, she was afraid of the dark.

Her fingers trembled as she reached for the light switch she had remembered seeing on the wall next to the bedroom door, relief flooding through her as the lights came on. The house felt quiet and still. She had pulled on her coat before leaving the bedroom rather than wear the folded but Finn-sized robe he had given her. There was something about the intimacy of wearing something that belonged to him that was far too potentially dangerous for her to risk. The brilliance of the chandelier illuminating the stairs made her blink a little. Quickly she padded down the stairs and into the hall. She was less than halfway across it when the drawing room door was suddenly flung open and Finn strode into the hall.

Like her, he must have been asleep. But unlike her he obviously had no hang-ups about semi-nudity—and no modesty either, Maggie decided shakily as she frantically tried to focus on something other than his naked torso, wondering what on earth was wrong with her recalcitrant gaze as it recklessly returned to his shorts-only clad body.

'Where the hell do you think you're going?'

The harshness of his angry demand bemused her, forcing her to lift her gaze to meet his in response to his angry challenge.

'I'm going for a drink of water,' Maggie responded.

'Dressed like that? Do you think I'm a complete fool?' he demanded without giving her any opportunity to answer. 'I appreciate how keen you are to leave, Maggie—'

'Leave…?' Maggie gave him a blank look. 'I'm not leaving.'

'Then why are you wearing your coat?' Finn asked her grimly

Her coat! Maggie had forgotten that she was wearing it. Pink with embarrassment, she shrugged as noncha-

lantly as she could as she told him, 'I…er…just put it
on to come downstairs in…you know…as a sort of a
robe. I'm not wearing my shoes,' she pointed out. 'Or…'
Self-consciously she stopped.

'Or…?' Finn prompted, recovering his sang-froid with
a speed she envied.

When she remained silent, he pressed her softly. 'If
you don't answer me, Maggie, then I'll have to use my
imagination, and right now it's telling me…' He stopped
and groaned before challenging her hoarsely, as he came
towards her, 'Have you any idea just what it's doing to
me knowing that you're as near as dammit naked underneath that coat?'

Maggie could feel her heart beating so frantically that
it literally shook her whole body. The effect the raw
sensuality of Finn's voice was having on her was making
it almost impossible for her to breathe. It shocked her
that she should feel so wantonly excited by the knowledge that Finn found her desirable, that he wanted her.
The voice of caution and common sense urged her to
say nothing, to walk away from temptation whilst she
still could. But when she responded it was to a far
stronger and more deeply rooted instinct, a contrary
reckless impulse impelling her to challenge him.

'If you're trying to tell me that you want me, then—'

'Then what?' Finn interrupted her rawly. 'Then you'd
rather I showed you?'

Maggie gasped as he caught hold of her, but not out
of shock or protest. No, it was her own reaction to him
that caused her to tremble so violently. She could feel

the rapid tattoo of Finn's heart, even through the muffling folds of her coat. But she wasn't feeling him through her coat at all, she recognised dizzily as Finn parted it and slid his hands inside it.

'Nothing,' she heard him whisper in a thick openly aroused voice. 'You aren't wearing anything at all.'

'I was in bed,' Maggie responded in a voice she had intended to be indignant but which in reality had become soft and slurred with reactive need.

'In bed...in my bed. Have you any idea how much I've been aching to be there with you?' Finn told her. 'Ever since...'

'Ever since I got here?' Maggie questioned, striving to keep her balance in the midst of a passion that was threatening to totally overwhelm her.

'No,' Finn told her starkly. 'Ever since you left it.'

It was too much. Helplessly Maggie gave in, closing her eyes in subjugation to her own feelings.

'There hasn't been a single night since then when I haven't wanted you,' Finn was whispering to her as he bent his head towards hers and slowly started to kiss her—slow, seductive kisses, strung together in an erotically dazzling chain that would tie her to him for ever, she suspected, as her body melted into his and his fingertips stroked her neck from her jaw to her collarbone, raising an erotic line of goosebumps that gave away her longing for him.

'Which is it to be?' she could hear Finn whispering as his lips found and then probed the warmth of hers. 'Your bed or mine? Mine's nearer... Or we could always try them both… The fire's still warm in the drawing room. Have you ever made love in front of a fire, Maggie, with the firelight highlighting every delicious inch of you, and your lover's body to keep you warm…?'

Maggie shuddered in mute pleasure at the images the hypnotic seduction of his voice was conjuring up for her. 'No…' Her denial was a strangled sound that tore at her throat, making her close her eyes against the acid burn of her own tears as she wondered how many other women Finn might have shared such a pleasure with, whilst she had never…

'No…? Oh, of course, I was forgetting. Open fires and city living don't exactly go together, do they?'

There was a harshness in his voice now that physically hurt her.

'I wouldn't know,' her honesty compelled her to tell him. 'Since I don't—I haven't… There isn't…' Her voice started to tail away. She didn't want to talk, to spend time dealing with the cumbersome delay of words, and she certainly didn't want to be forced to think about the other women who might have shared Finn's life. What she wanted, *all* she wanted… Maggie gave a small shiver as she tried to ignore what she was feeling. What was it that happened to her whenever she got physically close to Finn that affected her so strongly, that made her feel that what was happening between them was the most important thing in her life?

'What are you trying to tell me, Maggie?' Finn demanded grimly, cupping her face with his hands and looking down into her eyes so that there was no way she could hide her expression from him. 'That there hasn't been anyone else?' He gave her a derisive look. 'Do you really expect me to believe that a woman as intelligent, as desirable, as downright impossible to resist as both of us know you are, lives the life of a celibate?'

It frightened Maggie to realise how much pleasure it gave her to hear him describe her in such a way—and how much more the rawly sensual message in his eyes was giving her.

'I wanted to concentrate on my career,' she told him truthfully. 'And that hasn't left me any time for...for relationships.'

The way he was looking at her made her heart slam so heavily into her chest wall that she gasped out loud.

'Oh, Maggie...Maggie...'

She gasped again at the fierce note of male passion she could hear in Finn's voice as he slid his hands into her hair and bent his head to kiss her.

'You do things to me that no other woman has ever done, do you know that?' she heard Finn whispering passionately to her several minutes later as he raised his mouth from hers.

She could feel their breath mingling as he lowered his head again, and the fine tremors running through her body echoed the much fiercer shudders galvanising his.

Wrapped in one another's arms, they made their way slowly towards the drawing room, their journey there interspersed with fiercely passionate kisses and Maggie's softly breathy little moans of pleasure as Finn's hands caressed her naked body. But it was the sight of the firelight playing on his body as he released her briefly to remove the duvet from the sofa and place it in front of the fire that sent such wild surges of arousal through her that Maggie couldn't help herself from making a small strangled cry of longing.

'What is it?'

The look of frowning anxiety he gave her as he dropped the duvet and came towards her made her blush a little at the explicitness of her thoughts. And then, as though he had guessed them, his frown gave way to a look of heavy-lidded sensuality that made her bones feel as though they were melting as it skimmed lazily over her body, and a heat that had nothing whatsoever to do with the fire burned through her.

'Finn…' she protested, so shocked by her own desires that she immediately blamed him for causing them. Prior to knowing Finn she had lusted after a pair of new shoes far more strongly than she had ever lusted after a man— but now…

'Come here,' Finn commanded softly.

Helplessly Maggie went to him, knowing that he was not so much demanding something from her as giving her the right to take whatever she wished from him.

'City lady, country man,' Finn whispered to her as he smoothed her skin with his hands, making her shudder as rivulets of hot, swift delight ran over her. 'We're poles apart, and yet there's never been anyone I've ached so much to be close to.'

Awed by the intensity of the feeling she could hear in his voice, Maggie closed her eyes against the tight

ball of emotions she could feel blocking her throat.
When she could finally manage to speak all she could
say was a choked, 'Well, you are close to me now.'

'But not as close as I want to be,' Finn murmured as
his fingertips investigated the exquisite silky sensitivity
of her taut nipples. 'Skin on skin, body on body, mouth
on mouth. That's how close I want to be to you,
Maggie.'

She knew she must have made some reply because
she heard the sudden acceleration of Finn's breathing in
response to it, and then blissfully his mouth was on her
throat, trailing hot kisses of sheeting fire down her arm,
to the sensitive hollow of her elbow, nibbling at her fingers, licking and sucking them until she thought she
might actually faint with the intensity of the desire ex-
ploding inside her.

When he kneeled in front of her and kissed her waist,
the curve of her hip, her belly, Maggie moaned his name,
her fingers digging into the hard muscles of his arms as
she clung desperately to him, driven beyond shock by
the extent of her response to him, her need for him.
Through the haze of her longing she could see the long
weals her nails had raked against his skin. Mindlessly
she leaned into him, shuddering as his breath touched
her skin.

His hands were shaping her hips, stroking down the
length of her legs. Tenderly and carefully Finn lowered
her to the floor. As he leaned over her Maggie watched
him, her gaze drinking in the male perfection of him.
She lifted her hand to his shoulder, slowly tracing the

shape of his collarbone and then moving over his chest, exploring the tight hardness of his small male nipples with a wide-eyed concentration that made her soft brown eyes darken to almost black.

'How much longer are you going to torment me?'

The raw hunger in his low growl bit at her aroused emotions with the same devastating effect the erotic nibble of his teeth had had on her flesh. A thousand, no a million tiny sparks of hunger for him ignited at once, feeding a conflagration that threatened to totally overwhelm her.

Finn's fingers circled her ankle, slowly stroking its delicate bones. Maggie shivered and made a low guttural sound of shocked pleasure as he held her foot in both his hands and then slowly kissed its delicate instep. Immediately her toes curled in a rictus of female response.

'Me torment you?'

Maggie wasn't even aware of whispering the passion-husked words, nor of reaching towards him, pulling him against her, her hands trembling as they absorbed the hot velvet sleekness of his skin and the hardness of the muscles it cloaked.

They made love hungrily and fiercely, Finn holding Maggie's hips in a grip that was possessively hard as she straddled him, enjoying the power to dominate their intimacy and control the hot sleek strength of his body as it entered hers. Each stroke quickened the immediate response of her own flesh as she urged him to seek deeper, to stay longer, to move faster...harder, to give her everything that her body needed in order to satisfy the hunger for him he himself had created.

Her body was slick with sweat, arching against the taut bow of her orgasm, and Finn looked up into her face, drinking in the triumph of watching her succumb to her pleasure. The firelight gilded her damp skin, dancing in a million tiny flames as the shudders of completion convulsed her, and then it was his turn, the dying sound of his release fading into the mingled harshness of their joint breathing.

CHAPTER EIGHT

SLEEPILY Maggie turned over, savouring the warmth of Finn's bed. Finn himself was downstairs, where he had gone to make them both a cup of coffee. Maggie smiled to herself as she stretched with sensual luxury beneath the duvet. The warmth of Finn's bed wasn't all she was savouring. There was the warmth of Finn's body to be remembered as well, along with his lovemaking last night.

The tenderness he had shown her after the fierce intensity of the passion they had shared still had the power to raise a small frisson of emotional reaction from her as she mentally relived the way he had left her curled up in an exhausted tangle of limbs on the duvet, returning a few minutes later with two huge soft warm towels, gently drying her love damp body with one of them before tenderly wrapping the other around her.

Too relaxed to move, she had drifted off to sleep, waking only when he had kissed her and told her that he thought she would sleep more comfortably in his bed.

'Only if you share it with me,' she had answered.

She had woken at first light, whilst he was still asleep, lying next to him and savouring not just her memories of their lovemaking but the reality of his physical presence in bed beside her. Unable to stop herself, she had leaned across to him, studying his sleeping face, feeling the now familiar jolt run deliciously through her body as she'd given in to the temptation to stroke her finger-tips exploratively along his collarbone before tangling them gently in the silky warmth of the thick whorls of dark hair the night had flattened against his skin, whilst her lips had teased wake-up-and-play kisses in the hollow of his throat.

Seconds later, when he was still asleep, she had reluctantly been about to move away from him when he had made her almost jump out of her skin by growling mock threateningly at her at the same time as he imprisoned her in his arms, adroitly rolling her beneath him.

Somehow during the play-fight that had followed he had managed to stroke and kiss every sensually vulnerable bit of her.

'That's not fair,' she had pretended to complain when he had gently pinned her arms down at her sides so that she could not touch him, whilst his mouth had had the freedom to make an explosively erotic journey from her throat to both of her naked breasts. The sensation of his tongue lapping seductively at their rapidly hardening crests had made her arch her back in wild abandon, her protests forgotten, their game forgotten as desire had engulfed them both.

Maggie closed her eyes, and then opened them again as she heard Finn demanding softly, 'You haven't gone back to sleep, have you?'

Sitting up, she smiled at him, shaking her head. 'Is the snow still there?' she asked him.

He had been leaning towards her, having put down the tray he had been carrying, and she had lifted her face to his, anticipating his kiss. A little to her chagrin it never came, and instead he straightened up, glancing towards the window, his voice suddenly almost jarringly brisk. 'It's still there,' he confirmed. 'But it is thawing...'

Thawing. That meant that she would be able to leave. Ruefully Maggie acknowledged that a part of her would have been secretly glad if he had told her that they were likely to be snowed in together for several days.

'Breakfast,' Finn was telling her, indicating the tray he had placed on the bedside table next to her. 'And don't try going all city woman on me and telling me that you don't want any.'

Maggie deliberately evaded the tenderly teasing look he was giving her. Normally she did not eat breakfast, but whenever she was with Finn she woke up with the kind of appetite—for food—that would have pleased even someone as traditional as her grandmother, who had always insisted on Maggie eating what she termed a 'proper' breakfast before leaving the house in the morning.

That she also woke up with an even greater hunger for Finn himself was something she was most certainly not going to dwell on!

Turning to pick up a glass of orange juice from the tray, Maggie wondered how he was likely to react if she were to respond with the tongue-in-cheek comment that after a night like the one they had just spent together it was no wonder that she was hungry—for food, that was. So far as sensual satisfaction went her appetite should have been more than sated.

Her face started to grow slightly pink. The lethargy filling her body was a feeling that was entirely new to her, but then the lovemaking they had shared had also been something she had never imagined experiencing. Being brought up by her grandparents had given her a certain shy modesty which, no matter how much she might deplore it as being ridiculous in a sophisticated woman of her age, did make her feel slightly inhibited about talking openly about her most private feelings— especially when they were the kind of feelings that Finn aroused in her.

Lowering her gaze, she watched from beneath her lashes as Finn bit into a piece of toast. He had pulled on a robe before going downstairs, but he hadn't fastened it, and... Unable to help herself, Maggie peeped discreetly at his bare torso. Somehow, of its own accord, her glance slid lower, whilst her breathing stilled and then quickened, matching the fluttering thrill disturbing her heartbeat.

She thought that Finn wasn't aware of what she was doing but then she heard him advising her softly, 'Don't do that. Not unless you want me to...'

'I thought you said you had to go and see how the alpaca are,' Maggie reminded him quickly.

Not because she didn't want him, she acknowledged, hot-faced, but because—shockingly—she did.

'Hmm…had enough of me?' he teased her.

'No…never…' Maggie responded fervently, unable to check her vehement response.

However, before she could feel embarrassed by her self-betrayal, Finn was putting down his coffee to cup her face in his hands whilst he told her gruffly, 'That isn't the way to encourage me to go out and check on the livestock.'

Maggie held her breath until she felt the warm brush of his lips against hers, and then she exhaled in a soft shaky rush as his kiss deepened.

Her un-drunk coffee had gone cold by the time Finn finally left the bedroom, fully dressed to go and check on his animals.

Maggie got up at a more leisurely pace, blessing the properties of modern underwear that meant that it could be rinsed through to dry overnight. If there was one thing she should have learned from her recent experiences it was that whenever she came to Shropshire she ought to bring a change of clothes with her.

She was halfway downstairs when her mobile rang. Her caller was a client urgently needing to replace a key member of staff who had unexpectedly announced her intention to relocate to Boston to be with her lover.

Maggie had her laptop with her, and within minutes of ending the call she had drawn up a shortlist of potential replacements for her client and e-mailed them to him. Less than an hour later, seated in Finn's kitchen, drinking the cup of coffee she had just made herself, she was congratulating herself on the efficiency with which she had already set up the necessary interviews.

But it wasn't the speed with which she had been able to respond to her client's request that was exciting her so much that she was pacing the kitchen floor in eager anticipation, she acknowledged giddily. No, what was filling her with so much euphoria that she just could not keep still was the sudden realisation of just how easy it was for her to work without being in London. Of course, she argued to herself, if she were, to say, for instance, relocate to Shrewsbury, she would still need to keep up to date with her contacts in London. But if she organised things properly that could be done with regular bi-weekly meetings. Meetings that would still enable her to get home in the evening, of course...

Home...

She stopped mid-turn to stare out of the kitchen window. The snow was melting rapidly now, but it wasn't the snow that was commanding her attention.

Home... The tiny hairs on the back of her neck lifted in atavistic reaction to what she was thinking.

Home and Finn. Since when had the two become synonymous? Since when had Finn become so important to her, so vital to her, that he was her home? And when had she started to allow herself to acknowledge that fact? Since last night? Because they had made love? Or was it truer to say that those feelings had been there right from the very first time they had touched?

Then she had fought against them, determined to extinguish them, to deny and destroy them. Then she had been afraid of what admitting to them would mean, of how vulnerable it might make her. But now things were different. Something had changed. She had changed. Just how or why wasn't something she could in any way analyse, Maggie acknowledged in rueful mental defeat as she tried to apply her analytical faculties to the intensity of her emotions. Brainpower alone could not unravel the complexities of her feelings, her instincts, nor explain how or why her anger and her fear had somehow been transmuted into acceptance of her love, into a feeling which had begun as a tiny trickle but had been slowly gathering force within her right from the first moment they had met.

It was only now that she was able to recognise it for what it was—and it was totally revolutionising the way she looked at things. She was experiencing a need to admit into her life a cleansing surge of desire to sweep away her old repressions, the old barriers against love which she had clung to so fearfully. She was experiencing a sense of release and relief that was lifting from her the weight of a burden she hadn't previously known that she carried, and that burden had been a responsibility, an awareness of life as a serious affair, in which the self-indulgence of falling in love was a luxury she could not permit herself.

Unlike her parents, who had lived selfishly, hedonistically intent only on indulging themselves in the experience of the moment, without giving any thought to the feelings of others or the future, Maggie had felt that it was incumbent on her to behave more responsibly, suppressing her own emotions, crushing them, if necessary, in order to do so.

Now, illuminatingly, she could see that such extremes, such self-sacrifice was not necessary, that immaturity and selfishness on the part of her parents was to blame for what they had done, not love itself. She could see, too, that love and responsibility could work together, that commitment and independence could co-exist.

The first time she had told Finn she loved him she had hated herself and resented him in the backlash of fear that had immediately swamped her. Because of that she had told herself that she had been wrong, that she did not love him. But now she knew better. She ought to have listened to her heart all along. From now on... A happy smile curved her lips and Maggie started to hum beneath her breath. Then started to blush as she recognised that she was humming the 'Wedding March'.

A small gurgle of laughter bubbled in her throat. Knowing Finn as she was now coming to know him, she suspected that, had he heard her, been privy to her thoughts, he might well have suggested, with that special irresistibly tender teasing smile of his, that Handel's *Water Music*, the 'Triumphal March' he had written so beloved by the organisers of firework displays might have been a more appropriate tune for her to hum from his point of view!

Fifteen minutes later, when Finn walked into the kitchen, she was working busily on her laptop.

'Five minutes,' she told him. 'And then I'll be finished.'

As she spoke her mobile rang and she reached for it, her voice crisp and professional. 'Don't worry,' Maggie soothed as she listened to a girl she had only recently placed with one of the newer finance houses. 'If we're talking about sexual harassment then I'm prepared to speak personally to the chairman. I should be back in London by this evening. We can set up a breakfast meeting, if you like…'

As he stood behind her, listening to her, Finn's mouth compressed. What the hell was he doing, even allowing himself to think that they could share something? For him a long-distance affair, with Maggie in the City and him here in the country, could never work. It would be the emotional equivalent of snatching at fast food when he ached for something far more satisfying—for a meal he could linger over and savour in the same way he wanted to savour Maggie herself, and all that he felt for her. Those feelings could never be fulfilled by a brief series of meetings, nor compromised by being forced into that kind of mould. The way he felt about Maggie meant that he could never be content to be part of her life on a part-time basis.

Finn looked bleakly at her downbent head as she concentrated on her laptop. She was muttering to herself beneath her breath, so wholly engrossed in what she was doing that he might just as well not have been there.

Another few seconds and she would have finished, and then… Grimly, Maggie forced herself to recite under her breath what she was trying to do. If she didn't that aching longing she had to throw herself into Finn's arms and tell him just how she felt about him would overwhelm her and her work would be totally forgotten. She had her obligations, after all...

'There.' She sat back, exhaling in relief. 'All finished. How were the alpaca?' she asked Finn, smiling up at him as she turned round. 'Finn, what is it?' she asked anxiously, her smile fading as she saw his grim expression.

'This can't go on, Maggie,' Finn told her tersely.

He had to turn away from her as he spoke, knowing that if he looked directly at her he would betray what he was really feeling. And the last thing he wanted to do was to end up begging her to stay with him, to give up her life in London and share his. After all, he already knew what her answer to that would be.

The shock of his harsh words froze Maggie into numb silence. She knew if she tried to speak she would start to cry.

What she had expected, what she had longed to hear Finn say to her, was how much their night together had meant to him, how it had proved to him, as it had to her, that what they had was far too important to take second place in their lives. Like any woman in love she had wanted to hear the words that confirmed her feelings were shared, valued, reciprocated. She had wanted to hear Finn telling her that he loved her, that he never intended to let her go. Instead of which she could hear, and feel, the dull aching echo of his words pounding against her heart like blows.

Desperately she tried to reach out to him, unable to accept his rejection.

'Last night...' Her throat was so dry her protest sounded blurred and raw.

'Sexually the chemistry between us is explosive,' Finn interrupted her curtly. 'Neither of us can deny that. I've never—' He stopped, his face shadowed and grim.

'You've never what?' Maggie challenged him thickly, driven to impale herself even further on the sharp spears of anguish tearing into her heart, helpless to prevent herself from causing herself more pain. 'You've never met a woman more eager to go to bed with you?' She gave him a tight proud smile that defied him to look beyond it and see her pain. 'Enjoying sex for its own sake isn't a crime, is it? Men do it all the time.'

Inwardly she felt as though she was haemorrhaging the lifeblood of her heart, as though her emotions were being ripped apart. But there was no way she was going to let Finn guess how she felt. How could she have been so wrong about what they had shared? How could she have been so stupid as to imagine it was something special, something life-changing for him as it had been for her? Just because... Just because he had looked at her, touched her, made her think and feel that he cared...

Her hands were shaking so much she could hardly pack away her laptop. 'The snow's practically gone,' she told him. 'There's no reason for me to stay here any longer now.'

'Haven't you forgotten something?' Finn challenged her as she hurried towards the door.

Just for a moment she thought he had been teasing her, testing her, not realising just how devastating she found his inadvertent cruelty, but as she turned towards him, her body going weak with longing, she saw from his expression that whatever it was he intended to say it was most definitely not a declaration of love. Gritting her teeth together, she willed herself not to break down in front of him.

'Have I?' she responded quietly.

'We still haven't resolved the situation with the lease on the Dower House,' Finn reminded her.

He could think of that at a time like this?

What kind of fool was he? Finn demanded angrily of himself. He knew for his own sanity he couldn't afford the emotional risk of any future contact with her and yet here he was, clinging to the flimsiest excuse he could find to do so, knowing that with her grandmother living so close Maggie would have to visit.

Not knowing how on earth she was managing to keep her voice level, Maggie told him, 'You wanted to make it a condition of the lease that I never stayed in the Dower House with my non-existent lover. I'll agree to more than that for you, Finn. I'll agree never to stay there myself.'

'But you'll want to see your grandmother.' Finn frowned.

Did he think she might use the excuse of visiting her

grandmother to cloak a desire to see him? Only her pride was holding her together.

'Yes, I shall,' she agreed. 'But I don't have to inflict my unwanted presence on you in order to do that, Finn. I can, after all, see her in London.'

She was opening the door as she spoke, hurrying through the hall, ignoring the cold wet bite of the remaining snow as she pulled open the front door and walked through it to her car. There was still time for him to change his mind, to stop her from leaving, to reach for her and tell her that he just couldn't let her go. As she opened her car door Maggie held her breath.

He was standing by the open front door, so close that a few steps was all it would take for her to run back to him. Tears blurred her vision. What was it he had said to her? 'This can't go on...'

He couldn't have inflicted a more savage form of rejection on her, and he certainly couldn't have made it plainer how little he wanted to see her again. Faced with that knowledge she had no other option but to walk away from him in an attempt to keep her pride intact. Her pride was, after all, all she had left. Her heart was now ripped into ribbons of screaming unendurable pain.

CHAPTER NINE

SOON it would be Christmas. Maggie had her grand-mother's present all planned, providing her own and Finn's solicitors could get the lease for the Dower House drawn up and signed in time.

Finn.

Maggie had left Shropshire vowing that she would have no further contact with him, but then she had gone to visit her grandmother and had been shocked to see how frail, how fragile and unhappy she looked.

'I miss your grandfather so much,' she had told Maggie, adding quietly, 'This house seems so empty of everything that he was: his vibrancy, his sense of fun, his love of life. He was my strength, Maggie, and with-out him—'

She had stopped and looked away whilst Maggie's heart had rocked heavily against her chest wall.

Filled with fierce anxiety, Maggie had started to make plans—the foremost of them involving a letter to Finn over which she had pored with heart-wrenching inten-sity, imagining him receiving it, opening. Reading it.

The receipt of an e-mail from him had caught her off guard, but he had explained tersely at the end of it that the amount of work he was becoming involved in with the restoration of the house and the management of the farmlands had made the acquisition of a computer a necessity.

Knowing that her grandmother would be expecting her to spend the Christmas holiday period with her, as she always did, and knowing too that her grandmother would want to attend church on Christmas morning, and then no doubt to visit Maggie's grandfather's grave, Maggie had decided that even if the lease was through in time it might not be possible to travel to the Dower House over Christmas itself. Instead she was trying to compose a scrapbook of relevant information about both it and the early years of her grandparents' marriage to give to her grandmother on Christmas Day.

So far she had managed to surreptitiously extract from her grandmother's albums some photographs of them outside the Dower House, and the youth of their features had brought a huge lump to Maggie's throat as she'd studied their bright expectant expressions, their eyes full of a love for one another which not even the faded black and white photographs could dim.

Via their solicitors, Maggie had enquired of Finn if it would be possible to have an up-to-date photograph of the Dower House, explaining what she needed it for, but she was still awaiting his response.

Without giving anything away she had started to ask her grandmother about the early years of her marriage, hoping to glean from her conversation information which she could use to bring those special days back to life for her, to help banish some of the unhappiness she was now feeling.

Her mention of a favourite rose of her grandfather's had sent Maggie on a mission to acquire that same rose for the garden of the Dower House. Predictably it had been Gayle who had discovered a potential source of the rose for her, tracking down a company who specialised in growing traditional varieties. Maggie had gone to visit the company herself, to explain just why it was so important to her to obtain this particular rose, and to her joy they had confirmed that they were able to supply her with it, but had gone on to add that it would be 'bare root stock', explaining that this meant it would need to be planted immediately on delivery.

Maggie would have to wait until her grandmother had moved into the Dower House and planting conditions were right before sending it to her. However, in lieu of an actual plant, they had provided Maggie with a gift voucher inscribed with the name of the rose plus a brief history of it, to give to her grandmother.

Maggie had also borrowed a photograph of her grandfather at the age he had been when her grandparents had lived at the Dower House and had it secretly copied. She had hoped to be able to have her grandfather's image superimposed on a modern-day photograph of the Dower House, but this plan had to be put on hold until she had a response from Finn to her request for some photographs.

Gayle's helpful input into her plans had confirmed Maggie's view that her assistant was well deserving of the very generous bonus that Maggie was planning to surprise her with as an extra special 'thank you' for her hard work during the year.

It had shocked her, though, following Maggie's return to work, to hear Gayle commenting thoughtfully that she felt that Maggie had changed.

'Changed…in what way?' Maggie had demanded immediately.

'I'm not sure,' Gayle had admitted. 'It's just that you seem different somehow, less…driven,' she had explained semi-apologetically.

'Driven?' Maggie had tried not to look as taken aback as she'd felt. She had certainly always prided herself on her dedication to her career, but she did not find it complimentary to be described as 'driven'. But neither did she enjoy discovering that she was spending far too much time staring unhappily into space, fighting not to allow Finn to steal into her thoughts.

She had her career, her friends, her grandmother. Her plans. Surely she wasn't going to allow herself to feel that these were no longer enough for her just because… Just because what? Just because Finn didn't want her…because Finn didn't love her?

Maggie frowned as she reached for her coat. This evening she was dining with a client who wanted to discuss a possible new venture with her.

Bella Jensen was a feisty forty-something divorcee who had built up her small and extremely successful IT personnel business following the break-up of her marriage. She had had, as she had gleefully told Maggie, the very enjoyable pleasure of being approached by her ex-husband's company, who had come to her cap in hand to beg her to work under contract for them since, without the IT skills she had learned as the company had grown, they were lost.

Her husband had sold the small business they had built up together just prior to their break-up, brokering an excellent deal for himself, plus large consultancy fees, and claiming that Bella's contribution to the business had been negligible. She had been delighted—not just to be able to prove him wrong, but to have her importance to their business recognised publicly in a professional and financial manner.

From that experience she had gone on to recognise a growing need for skilled IT staff to work on a contract basis in various mainstream industries, and she had used Maggie's skills in the past to coax highly trained people onto her books.

Maggie liked her, and normally she would have been looking forward to spending an evening in her company. But right now she seemed to have lost the ability to enjoy anything. Right now it felt as though the whole of her life, not just the present but the future as well, had been blighted—and why?

Did she really need to ask herself that?

It was hard for her to fight against seeing in Finn's rejection of her an echo of her parents' earlier failure to truly love her. But that was to think of herself as a victim, and there was no way she was ever going to let herself be that.

Predictably, Bella had chosen one of London's current

crop of 'hot' eateries for them to have dinner in—the restaurant in the kind of superb hotel that people spoke about in hushed, awed voices.

'Love the outfit,' Bella commented enthusiastically to Maggie as they exchanged warm hugs in the foyer before going through to the restaurant. 'And you've lost weight,' she added accusingly, as they were shown to their table. 'I've joined a Pilates exercise course, but so far I have only managed one class,' she admitted ruefully as they both studied their menus.

The restaurant was busy, and Maggie gave a discreet glance at the other diners, recognising several well-known faces from television and the media.

'You said you had a new venture you wanted to talk over with me?' she reminded Bella.

'Mmm... You know, of course, that with the arrival of so many American banks in the City there's been an awful lot of transatlantic movement in the executive arena?'

Maggie nodded her head and waited.

'Over half my staff now are ex-Silicon Valley, and I'm seriously thinking about relocating my business to the USA. I'd have to take on an American partner, but that's all in hand, and what I wondered, Maggie, is whether or not you would be interested in taking over those of my people who want to remain UK-based.'

Maggie frowned. 'Bella, I'm a headhunter, not...'

'Don't turn me down yet. Think about it,' Bella started to cajole determinedly. 'You've got the people skills to do it, Maggie, and I can't think of anyone who would look after my people's interests better. Financially you'd do very well out of it, too. Of course, theoretically, one should be able to work from anywhere in the world with all this modern technology, and the fact that I'm going to be based in the States should not make any difference at all, but my people are very valuable commodities, with extremely fragile egos in some cases, that require a certain amount of hands-on attention. And that's something you are very good at, Maggie. What I'd got in mind for us was a partnership whereby— Wow!'

Bella broke off the earnestness of her discussion to say breathlessly, 'Just look over there—that table for two to our right. Mmm.' She sighed appreciatively. 'There's nothing quite like a big sexy man for making a woman remember that she's a woman, and he's very definitely all man and more.'

As she glanced idly in the direction Bella was indicating Maggie froze in shocked disbelief. The man Bella was drooling over was Finn. Finn, here in London, the place he abhorred, and sharing an intimate dinner with the kind of woman he supposedly found least attractive: a stunning, elegant, city-sleek brunette who was right now leaning across their table to place her hand over his whilst she smiled up into his eyes with the kind of smile that...

'Maggie? Are you okay?'

Somehow she managed to swallow down the fiery ball of mingled fury and pain lodged in her throat; somehow she managed to drag her furious and anguished gaze away from the two people who were so patently oblivious to her presence.

'Yes, yes, I'm fine,' she lied, adding desperately, 'Look, Bella, I'm afraid I'm going to have to cut and run. I forgot when we fixed dinner that I'd got something else on.'

As she spoke Maggie was standing up, desperate to leave the restaurant before Finn saw her, desperate to escape from that intimate little tableau that would be burned across her heart for ever.

Bella was looking confused, as well she might, Maggie acknowledged, and pressing her to think about the proposal she had outlined to her.

'Yes. Yes, I will,' Maggie promised her.

Oh, please God, let her get away before Finn saw her. Please, please, please…

Finn tried not to show his impatience as his solicitor outlined some of the problems she had been having in drawing up the lease for the Dower House. Maggie's request for some photographs of the house had led to him spending a bright afternoon photographing it, both inside and out, and the prints were now carefully tucked away in his briefcase, awaiting delivery to Maggie herself—his personal delivery. He could, of course, have mailed them, but since he had had to meet with his solicitor anyway, it had seemed only sensible to pass on the photographs to Maggie at the same time.

'I can't believe I've finally got you to come to London,' Tina was teasing him ruefully, leaning across the table to tap the back of his hand in light admonition when he made no response. 'Hello, Finn? Are you there?' she asked him dryly.

'I'm sorry,' he apologised. 'You were saying…?'

'I've checked with Paul about the lease, and we think we've finally ironed out all the potential problems.'

Paul was her husband and partner, and Finn had first got to know them when he himself had worked in the City.

'Oh, by the way, you'll never guess what. We're actually thinking of relocating ourselves. Paul's dealt with so many country conveyances for our clients recently that he's got itchy feet—'

She broke off her conversation as the sound of a chair being scraped back over the immaculate wooden floor broke the hushed silence of the restaurant. Automatically both of them looked in the direction of the sound.

Maggie…here…Finn couldn't believe it. He started to get up from the table, but Maggie was already heading for the exit.

'Finn, what is it?' Tina was asking him in bemusement.

'Nothing…I don't want to rush you, Tina, but there's someone else I have to see this evening.'

Maggie… Finn could feel his heart thudding heavily. Her dinner companion had been another woman and he knew he ought to be ashamed to admit just how much that pleased him.

The ache of missing her that had become a permanent feature of his life sharpened to a raging agony of need.

If loving her was hell, then living without her was even worse. But a part-time relationship, taking second place to her career, that would never be enough for him.

He wanted her to want him, to love him with the same degree of commitment and intensity he did her.

Picking up the papers Tina had given him, he opened his briefcase to put them inside. Beneath the wallet of prints of the Dower House lay a small sheaf of estate agents' brochures—one-bedroomed city apartments, *pièd-a-terres* just in case Maggie should...

Snapping his briefcase shut, he leaned over to kiss Tina.

He hadn't alerted Maggie to the fact that he intended to call and see her just in case she refused to see him. Outside the hotel he gave the taxi driver her address and prayed grimly that she would have gone home when she left the restaurant, and not on to another venue.

Just as soon as she had put down her coat and bag and kicked off her shoes, Maggie started to rifle through the contents of her kitchen cupboard and fridge, with the panicky desperation of an addict hunting for a fix. It didn't matter that she already had a freezer full of chilli; the need to make some more gripped her in its frantic compulsion. Making chilli soothed and comforted her, and it reminded her too that she was an independent strong-minded woman who could do anything she wished.

Except stop loving Finn.

Her frenzied movements ceased, her body going still

and then stiff as her doorbell rang. It would probably be her neighbour, wanting to talk through the problems with her current relationship Maggie decided as she unlocked and opened the door.

Only it wasn't her neighbour—it was Finn...

Grimly she wondered how on earth he had got past Bill, the supposedly impenetrable barrier against unwanted and uninvited visitors in whom her grandmother placed such faith.

Finn, guessing what she might be thinking, reflected ruefully on the very imaginative 'sweetener' he had been forced to offer the doorman, along with an equally imaginative sob story, in order to gain access to the building.

'It's more than my life's worth to let you in without checking that you're expected, guv,' had been his initial reaction to Finn's arrival in the hallway.

Finn just hoped that if she ever got to know the truth Maggie's grandmother would forgive him for taking not just her name in vain, as it were, but also for the totally fictitious friendship with her which he had claimed which, even more than the money he had handed over, had swayed the Cerberus guarding the doorway in his favour.

Weakly Maggie gave in to her own need and looked hungrily at him. The city suit and crisp shirt he was wearing emphasised the country hardness of his body with its lean muscular strength.

Shakily she stepped back from the door. There was a small betraying smear of lipstick on his cheek. Unable to stop herself, she focused on it, all too easily imagining the seductive manner in which the brunette would have coaxed him to stay with her.

'I've got some photographs for you—of the Dower House,' Finn was saying as he pushed her front door shut. 'I was a bit concerned that they might get lost in the post, so I decided to deliver them myself. I had to come to London anyway, to see someone...'

'Yes, I saw you with her in the restaurant,' Maggie told him fiercely whilst her brain fought to regain control of her tongue from her wildly out of control emotions— and lost—with a vengeance. 'Obviously some city women do meet with your approval,' she heard herself saying challengingly. Then, as her brain cut in, before she could betray herself even further, 'I'd like you to leave please,' she added quickly.

'Leave?' Finn questioned. 'But...'

'Yes, leave,' Maggie confirmed. 'And right now.'

Somehow she managed to angle her way past him in the small hallway, and as she reached for the front door handle the pain driving her forced her to say acidly, 'Fortunately in the City we aren't subject to impassable fords or impenetrable blizzards, so on this occasion there won't be any need— Oh!' She gave a shocked gasp as without warning the flat was plunged into complete darkness.

Her fiercely guarded and secret fear of the dark was a hangover from her childhood which mortified her, but as the darkness blacked out every single particle of light she could feel the panic caused by the inky blackness of the windowless hallway roaring through her.

Frantically she tried to cling to her self-control. 'It must be a fuse,' she heard herself saying weakly to Finn as she stood rooted to the spot, terrified of moving.

'More like a power blackout,' she could hear him responding grimly. She could tell from his voice and the emptiness of the air close to her that he had moved away from her and into her living room. From there he called out to her. 'Everything's in darkness. I can't see a light anywhere.'

Everything. No lights. Not anywhere. Maggie could feel herself starting to tremble violently, but from somewhere she managed to find the strength of will to claim denyingly, 'This is the City; we don't have power blackouts.'

'Mmm…like fords don't flood and heavy snow doesn't fall in November,' Finn agreed sardonically. 'Well, whether you like it or not, there's no way I'm leaving you here on your own until the power returns.'

Shamingly, the first reaction Maggie had to his announcement was one of intense relief. To punish herself for it, she said grittily, 'I'm sure your dinner companion would be a much more suitable candidate for your company than me.'

'Tina?' Finn questioned. 'She's my solicitor. She and her husband Paul are old friends from my City days.'

His solicitor. Now Maggie was actually grateful for the darkness, to protect not just her hot flush of embarrassment but, more importantly, the almost intoxicatingly intense quiver of happiness that shot through her.

Even so, she still insisted, 'There really isn't any need for you to stay.'

'If you think for one minute that I'm going to leave you here on your own in a situation like this—'

Maggie's heart started to thud even more anxiously as she listened to him. If Finn were to leave now, Maggie knew that she would remain curled up right here in her small hallway until the power returned or it grew light. That was how afraid of the dark she was.

'Do you have any candles?' Finn was demanding.

'Yes… Yes, I do. They're…they're in the kitchen.' She swallowed nervously at the thought of having to make her way through the thick darkness of her flat to her kitchen. She would rather stay where she was.

She waited, dry-mouthed, for Finn to insist that she got the candles, and her legs weakened dangerously when instead he told her, 'Let's go and get them, then. You lead the way.'

And then, as he finished speaking, he reached for her hand, holding it in the warm grip of his own.

Oh, the blessed relief of that lovely warm human contact. Maggie closed her eyes and took a deep steadying breath. She could actually feel Finn's presence surrounding her, protecting her, giving her the courage and the strength to urge her shaky legs to move her towards the kitchen.

She could feel Finn standing behind her as she opened the kitchen cupboard where she kept her dinner candles. The matches were with them, and as she turned round to hand everything to Finn the discovery that he was standing so close to her that her movement had brought them body to body caused her to shake so much that she dropped the matches.

They both bent down to retrieve them at the same time and Maggie could feel the warmth of Finn's breath against her face. An aching wanton yearning for him filled her. Fiercely she fought against it.

He might be doing the correct gentlemanly thing now, in insisting on remaining with her, but she was not going to let herself fall into the delusion of thinking that it meant anything—especially the kind of 'anything' that might have her telling him about how she had had a change of heart about the absolute necessity of her living in the City, or how she could now see that it would be possible for her to live in the country and still continue to run her business. And she certainly wasn't going to tell him of the long lonely empty nights she had lived through since her return to London, nor the way that in her darkest hours she would have given anything, everything, just to be with him. Just to be held in his arms close to him. Just to be sharing the intimacy of his bed with him, wrapped in the even more precious intimacy of his arms…his love.

She tensed as she heard the rasp of a match, her eyes widening as she saw Finn's face briefly outlined in the quick flare before he protected the flame with his hand and lit the candles.

What was it about candlelight that immediately gave even the most mundane of surroundings an aura of sensuality and romance? As they both stood up, Maggie could see the way Finn looked round her kitchen.

'You're cooking chilli?' he questioned her frowningly.

'Is there any reason why I shouldn't?' Maggie responded in immediate self-defence. 'I happen to like it. Not that it's any business of yours.'

'I should hope you do,' Finn agreed, ignoring the final challenging sentence of her response. 'There's enough stuff here to feed a small army. I trust you've taught yourself how to cook mince in the last few months?'

His frown deepened, and he stared at her for so long that Maggie felt slightly nervous. 'You aren't wearing any shoes,' Finn told her, and his frown gave way to a look of wondering male amusement as he grinned. 'You're tiny.'

'I am no such thing,' Maggie denied indignantly.

'Oh, yes you are.' Finn contradicted her softly. 'Tiny and stubborn and...' Putting the newly lit candles down on the worktop, he moved purposefully towards her.

Immediately Maggie panicked, moving back from him, knocking over the candles as she did so. The small flames were instantly extinguished.

The effect of the darkness on her already sensitive nervous system caused her to cry out, a small choked sound of distress which Finn reacted to, demanding, 'Maggie, what is it? Are you all right?'

'No, I'm not all right,' Maggie burst out. 'I hate the dark. It makes me feel so afraid.'

In the silence that followed her small outburst, Maggie

cursed her reckless tongue. What on earth had she told him that for? He would think she was a complete fool. And yet despite that she still heard herself continuing, in a distinctly wobbly little voice.

'It frightens me and...'

Before she could finish Finn was saying gruffly, 'I hate spiders. They terrify me. I have nightmares about them...'

In the darkness Maggie listened to his breathing. The thought of Finn being afraid of anything—and admitting that fear to her—brought a warm rushing flood of protective love washing through her.

'At least you can do something about the darkness. Spiders are there all the time,' Finn told her.

Without thinking about what she was doing, Maggie took a step towards him.

'How about you protecting me from spiders whilst I protect you from the dark?' Finn suggested.

Finn must have moved too, because now his voice was right against her ear, and his arm was right round her waist, and his lips...

'Do you think that's really a good idea?' Maggie whispered. With Finn's lips deliberately teasing hers it was almost impossible for her to think, never mind speak.

'Mmm. And I think that this is an even better idea,' Finn muttered as his arms wrapped round her and he began to kiss her in earnest.

Maggie could feel her head starting to swim whilst

her body melted with the sweet wanton pleasure of being so close to him.

'Oh, God, Maggie, if you only knew how much I've missed you. How much I've wanted you,' she could hear Finn groaning hoarsely to her.

The only response she could make was to wrap her own arms around him and open her mouth to the hot seeking pressure of his tongue. Behind the closed velvet of her eyes the darkness beyond them didn't matter, because she could see in her mind's eye all that she wanted to see. And that was Finn. Her fingertips touched his face, tracing its bone structure, and she felt her body thrill with the unexpected sensuality of the tension in his jaw as she stroked his skin.

With an urgency that both shocked and thrilled her Finn was unfastening her clothes, his whole body shuddering sharply when he touched her bare skin.

'God, you feel so good,' he moaned against her throat. 'The scent of you in my bed has been driving me crazy, do you know that? Every time I've closed my eyes all I've seen is you, all I've wanted to touch is you. You are the air I breathe, Maggie, every thought I think…my heart…my soul.'

Maggie gasped and trembled as his hand cupped her naked breast.

'Undress me, Maggie. Take me to bed, show me that you want me. Be the wild wanton woman I know you can be, the woman who isn't afraid to put love first in her life.'

His hoarse words filled her heart with a hot vocal

torrent of fiercely moaned desire, challenging her to meet and match his need.

'Right now nothing is more important to me than you...and this,' Finn was telling her roughly. 'Kiss me, Maggie. Show me that you want me,' he begged her, but before she could move he was kissing her, taking her mouth with shockingly intense hunger.

The darkness, for so many years her dreaded, hidden and feared enemy, had suddenly become a welcome sensual cloak within which she could hide from any danger of exposure, be free to respond with every bit of the rich sensuality of her true nature to what he was demanding of her.

They made love quickly and passionately, tearing at buttons and fastenings, the raw broken sound of their frantic breathing interrupted by the sharp moan of pleasure Maggie gave when Finn lifted her onto the worktop and sank into her. Until she had felt him there even she hadn't realised how much she had longed for the fulfilment of his possession, how much her body had ached for the feel of him within it.

His own release followed hers, flooding through her as the final shimmering pulsations of her orgasm died away.

As he lifted her off the worktop Finn crooned her name between gentle kisses whilst Maggie tried to stop her body from trembling with the shocked aftermath of what had happened.

'Maggie, Maggie...' Finn was cupping her face, stroking his thumbs over her cheekbones, still damp with the release of her orgasmic tears. 'I want...'

They both blinked as the power suddenly came back on. Maggie could see scratches on Finn's bare shoulder, which she must have inflicted in the heat of their passion. The kitchen floor was strewn with discarded clothes and the air smelled of passion—and Finn. She was appalled by the ferocity of her longing to beg him to stay. To tell him that she would do anything, be anything, in order to share her life with him. The intensity of her emotions made her feel physically weak. She wanted to crawl into bed and pull the covers up over her head. No, what she really wanted was to go to bed with Finn and to curl up there against his body whilst he held her and told her how much he loved her.

But he didn't love her.

Unable to endure looking at him, she quickly pulled on her scattered clothes and told him disjointedly, 'You can't stay here. I want you to leave...'

Like her, Finn had finished dressing.

'Maggie—' he began, but Maggie couldn't bear to listen; she was so close to breaking down completely and begging him to let her into his life. Skirting past him, she walked into her sitting room.

Finn followed her, mentally cursing himself beneath his breath. No wonder she wanted him to leave after the way he had behaved. Why the hell hadn't he taken things more slowly? Did he really need to ask himself that? The sight of her, the scent of her, the reality of her had turned the final screw in the already over tightly coiled ferocity of his need and he had totally lost control. Even now, just thinking about the way she had felt when he had sunk into her, the receptive warm wetness of her, the...

She was walking across the sitting room, heading for the hallway, obviously determined to make him leave.

'Maggie...wait...I've got the draft lease here for you to look at. Tina gave it to me earlier. And those photographs I was telling you about...' As he spoke Finn was reaching for his briefcase and opening it.

Reluctantly Maggie turned round and watched him. In his desperation Finn accidentally dropped the case, spilling its contents. Maggie watched in silence as he gathered up the spilled papers and then tensed as she saw the estate agents' brochures. 'You're thinking of buying a London flat?' she demanded, unable to conceal her shock.

For a moment Finn was tempted to lie and tell her he had got them for a friend, but what was the point?

'I was,' he acknowledged, giving her a grimly wry look. 'Like I've told you before, Maggie, a part-time relationship with you isn't what I want. I thought it was better to let you go completely rather than be forced to life on the fringes of your life, fitted in between business deals, always knowing that I came a poor second best, that my love for you came second best. But the way I've been feeling these last few weeks has changed my mind, and one of the reasons I came to London was to see you and to tell you...to ask you...if it would make any difference to…to things if I were prepared to spend a couple of nights a week in London. That way—'

Maggie didn't let him finish. 'You'd do that for me?' she asked him quietly. 'You'd buy a flat in London just so that you could see me…?'

The tremor in her voice and the look in her eyes made Finn's heart ricochet against his chest wall. 'To have your love, Maggie, I'd—' He stopped and drew a deep breath before admitting huskily, 'I'd do whatever it takes. Living in the City might be one kind of hell as far as I'm concerned, but living without you is every kind of hell there is and then some, all rolled into one unbearable pain.'

'Oh, Finn.'

He gave a small grunt as he exhaled when she threw herself into his arms, but he still had the presence of mind to lock them around her and to kiss her with fiercely sweet passion before asking her hoarsely, 'Will you do it, Maggie? Will you let me into your life, share your time and yourself with me?'

'For two nights a week whilst you're in London?' Maggie questioned him, gravely looking up into his eyes.

The hope and the pain she could see there tore at her own heart. He might not have said the words 'I love you', but he didn't need to; she could see his love in that expression.

'Yes. Will you?' he repeated thickly.

Very slowly Maggie shook her head.

'No,' she told him quietly.

'No…' He had gone white with shock, anguish written—no, carved into his face, Maggie recognised on a wave of sweetly tender love. 'Maggie…' he began, but she stopped him, placing her finger against his lips.

'No, Finn, you've had your say,' she told him gently, 'now it's my turn. I was so jealous tonight when I saw you in the restaurant, and so…so very unhappy when you told me that things couldn't go on between us. Do you remember…when we were snowed in?' she reminded him, watching his face.

'I can remember saying something, feeling…knowing that I'd go mad if I couldn't find some way of us reaching a compromise that would allow us to be together as lovers rather than adversaries,' Finn agreed.

'I thought you were telling me that you didn't want me,' Maggie whispered. 'I'd been waiting for you to come back from the animals so that I could tell you…'

She paused and played with his fingers, before running her own a little nervously up and down his arm whilst he clenched his muscles beneath the innocent seduction of her touch and begged her though gritted teeth, 'Maggie…?'

'Sorry,' she apologised, her face suddenly pink. 'I didn't mean… It's just that I love to touch you so much,' she told him.

'Maggie.' This time the warning in his voice was almost a groan.

'Oh, yes,' Maggie resumed hastily. 'Well, whilst you were out I'd been thinking that I could work quite easily from Shropshire…' She looked up into his face again, and then looked away quickly, telling him shakily, 'Don't do that, Finn, or I'll never be able to finish.'

'Why didn't you say something to me? Tell me?' Finn growled in despair.

'I...you seemed to be rejecting me,' was all that Maggie could say.

'Rejecting you...' Finn closed his eyes and breathed very deeply. 'After the way we'd just made love? Some rejection, Maggie. Are you really telling me that we've wasted the last four weeks living apart when we could have been together?' he demanded. 'That I've spent every single day and every single night aching for you...wanting you. God, those nights, Maggie. Have you any idea...?'

'Yes,' Maggie admitted frankly. 'Every idea!' She was still trying to come to terms with the sheer sweetness of the pleasure of knowing how much he loved her. It was making her feel giddy with its power and awesomeness.

'You'd really be prepared to work from Shropshire to be with me?' Finn was demanding gruffly in a voice that said he hardly dared believe what he was hearing.

'It makes very good economic sense,' Maggie told him demurely. 'Everyone who's anyone is downscaling these days, putting their private lives first. In my job it's important for me to be completely in tune with the needs and aspirations of my clients...'

'And so it's a business decision, is it?' Finn challenged her.

'Not entirely.' Maggie breathed in ecstatic pleasure as

he started to nibble teasing kisses along her jaw. Her eyes, which had been closed, suddenly opened as she tensed and demanded anxiously, 'I won't have to wear boots, will I, Finn? Well, I won't anyway. Not—'

'Not unless they have a designer label?' Finn supplied, tongue in cheek.

'Mmm,' Maggie sighed in soft pleasure as he started to kiss her.

'Mmm…' Finn agreed as his own voice thickened in urgent male need.

'Finn, what on earth are you doing?' Maggie demanded. They had been married just over six hours, both of them sharing a secret laughing look as they had walked down the aisle and out of the church to the victorious sound of Handel's 'Triumphal March'—Maggie having told Finn of her thoughts and feelings as she had waited for him to return to the house the morning before their fateful misunderstanding.

Now, having driven her grandmother back to the Dower House from their reception, they were supposed to be on their way to the airport to catch the flight for their tropical honeymoon destination. But instead of driving towards the airport, Finn was…Finn was…

Maggie stared in disbelief as she looked down from the window of Finn's new four-wheel drive to see that Finn was driving down towards the ford where they had first met.

When he stopped the car in the middle of its now gentle flow Maggie stared accusingly at him. She was wearing her going-away outfit, which just happened to be a raw silk white trouser suit with, of course, a pair of her favourite delicate stilettos.

'The first time we met here there was something I wanted to do that I've regretted not doing ever since,' Finn drawled.

There was a wicked glint in his eye that made Maggie's heart beat fast in female excitement.

'Oh, and what might that have been?' she teased him dulcetly, thinking that she could already guess. Perhaps if he had kissed her then it might have cut short a lot of later unhappiness, but from that they had both learned the value of loving compromise, and now they both respected one another and were equal partners in their relationship.

'This,' Finn told her promptly as he got out and went round to her door, splashing through the shallow ford as he did so. As he opened her door for her Maggie willingly allowed him to lift her out, laughing down into his eyes, but her laughter was replaced with a shocked gasp of indignation when, instead of kissing her, he smacked her firmly on her neat raw-silk-covered behind instead.

'Finn—' she began to protest indignantly, in proper female objection—although he hadn't actually hurt her, and there had been far more sensuality in his light touch than any real anger. But now he was kissing her and kissing her, with a hungry, tender loving passion that totally melted away her ire.

'And this...' he told her. 'How could you have been foolish enough to risk your pretty, wonderful, irreplaceable neck trying to cross that flood in that ridiculous city car? When I think what could have happened,' he groaned, and then checked, lifting his mouth from hers as Maggie let out a wail. 'What is it?' he demanded anxiously.

'My shoes,' she told him. 'They've fallen off...'

'Good. Now you'll never be able to escape from me,' Finn told her promptly as he lifted her back into the car. Maggie whispered something in his ear.

'Barefoot and what?' he demanded.

'You heard me.' Maggie laughed. 'And anyway,' she told him truthfully, 'I'll never want to escape, Finn. I love you too much.'

'No more than I love you,' he told her softly.

'Gran's so happy in the Dower House,' she said, smiling, when he had turned the round and they were heading for the airport.

'Mmm...and she's going to be even happier when we get back from honeymoon and tell her our good news,' Finn agreed.

Lovingly they exchanged tender private glances. The discovery that Maggie was pregnant was still too new and precious to share with anyone else. It was, as Finn had told her emotionally only that morning, the most wonderful gift of love she could possibly have given him—apart from herself.

'Like I said,' Maggie reminded him. 'You're an old-fashioned country type who wants to keep his woman barefoot and pregnant!'

'No,' Finn corrected her lovingly. 'What I want—all I want—is to keep you happy, Maggie.'

'Right,' the zephyr announced, dusting her hands together as she peered over the newest recruit's wing. 'That's those two sorted out. So who's next…?'

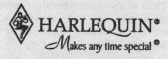

Coming Next Month

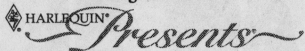

HARLEQUIN *Presents*

THE BEST HAS JUST GOTTEN BETTER!

HPCNM0202